Also by Beth Ain

Izzy Kline Has Butterflies

THE CURE

for

Cold Feet

a novel
in small moments

WITHDRAWN

beth ain

Random House · New York

Text copyright © 2018 by Beth Ain
Jacket art copyright © 2018 by Julia Denos

All rights reserved. Published in the United States by Random House Children's Books, a division of Penguin Random House LLC, New York.

Random House and the colophon are registered trademarks of Penguin Random House LLC.

Visit us on the Web! rhcbooks.com

Educators and librarians, for a variety of teaching tools, visit us at RHTeachersLibrarians.com

Library of Congress Cataloging-in-Publication Data
Names: Ain, Beth Levine, author.
Title: The cure for cold feet / Beth Ain.
Description: First edition. | New York : Random House, [2018] | Sequel to: Izzy Kline has butterflies. | Summary: Now in sixth grade, Izzy continues to face the ups and downs of everyday life in middle school, including dances, her brother's increasing distance, and her father's serious relationship.
Identifiers: LCCN 2017003384 | ISBN 978-0-399-55084-3 (hardcover) | ISBN 978-0-399-55086-7 (ebook)
Subjects: | CYAC: Novels in verse. | Middle schools—Fiction. | Schools—Fiction. | Friendship—Fiction. | Family problems—Fiction.
Classification: LCC PZ7.5.A39 Cu 2018 | DDC [Fic]—dc23

Printed in the United States of America
10 9 8 7 6 5 4 3 2 1
First Edition

Random House Children's Books
supports the First Amendment and celebrates the right to read.

For Grace,
music-maker,
snort-laugher,
truth-teller,
you float like a feather,
in a beautiful world.

Middle of Nowhere

They say middle school is
THE WORST.
Everyone says this.
Literally.
(Everyone also says *literally*.)
Mom's new best friend stopped by to say this thing
just tonight.
The night before the first day of
middle school.
Are you excited? she asks,
all lit up,
in the middle of dinner.
Are you ready? she asks five minutes later,
in the middle of my sentence about
NOT BEING READY.

Did you pick out a new outfit? she asks,

sweetly,

in the

middle of dessert.

I roll my eyes.

A new attitude? she asks, looking at me out of the sides

of her eyes.

Mom's new best friend is a yogi,

a person who teaches yoga and wears yoga bracelets,

and leggings, and leg warmers that go all the way up

to the

middle of her thighs.

Middle things everywhere.

Mom's new best friend is Jasmine Allen,

also known as

Jackson Allen's mom.

JACKSON ALLEN,

who is one of FOUR ANNOYING BOYS

who made their way through all of elementary school

as an ANNOYING gang of finger-slamming people

who made fun of any other person

who got

in the
middle of it
somehow.
Jackson is super excited, she says.
He's at his dad's tonight, but super, super excited.
I wish I were at MY dad's tonight, I think
in the
middle of her third *super.*
Middle school is not
THE WORST, I think.
She is.

Drama

Quinn Mitchell is mostly worried about not knowing
anyone all over again.
But you know ME, I insist,
thinking I am more than enough.
Dad always says I am A LOT.
And you know Lilly, I say,
putting my arm around good old Lilly's neck.
Lilly, who has two *ll*'s where there should be one, like
the flower. Lilly, whose second *l* turned out to be the
least of her quirks.
And you can open your locker, Lilly says,
doing her part now.
Think about me! I scream,
half kidding.
Think about your poor friend Izzy, who is—

I fake a sob—
lock challenged.
I fall in a heap on the floor of her room.
My part.
I have become an actress in the last year,
says my mom,
who made sure I got extra singing and acting lessons
after I sang and acted in
Free to Be . . . You and Me
in fourth grade,
a part given to me at the last minute by good old Lilly
and only because she got sick that day.
Quinn and Lilly and I became the best of friends that
year, a little late in the game—
partly because Fiona and Sara had taken up all my
friendship until then,
when they
left me behind
in part for soccer and dance and
in part for
too many other things to count.
Lilly turned Quinn and me from a twosome into a
threesome late that fourth-grade year.

Partly I felt guilty for stealing Lilly's song, and
partly I did not,
because I see now we were meant to be.
Three people who didn't fit anywhere
in particular but together.
A friendship,
in three parts.

Long Division

The lunchroom is loud and there are long tables
everywhere, waiting to be filled up with long groups
of sixth graders
and their lunch trays,
their water bottles
spilling out of
insulated lunch bags.
But there are only two of us standing here,
insulating each other.
We won't take up more than two-twelfths of a long table.
One-third of us is in another lunch period.
One-third of us is Lilly, with two *l*'s and only one of
everything else,
who has to fend for herself, and it is hard enough to
do this in twos.

I see a long table filled with
girls I have seen before,
girls who look more alike than not alike,
girls who have flashy smiles and bounce around each
other before settling
evenly
into their spots, where they
divide
and conquer.
I picture them with a
bracket around them.
12 into 12
is 1,
no remainders.
We don't fit.
We are divisors without a
dividend.
We will stay 2 at least until recess,
leaving space enough between our table and their
table to remain
intact,
one whole number,
prime for whatever comes—

division,
addition,
multiplication,
or subtraction.

Markers

Señora Navalón speaks with feeling,
even when she writes
¡La clase de la Señora Navalón!
in dry-erase marker on the first day of Spanish class.
She bangs the marker so hard against the board that it
shakes a little,
rattling the other markers
in their holder.
Rattling me awake too.
Spanish, I find, is the opposite of Hebrew,
which is the only other language I have ever tried
to learn,
and which doesn't even try to resemble English.
Hebrew looks to me, early on a Sunday morning,
at some uncivilized time,

when I can barely speak any language
at all,
more like the hieroglyphics I learned about last
period,
in social studies.
Social studies. Where we will study
civilizations
this year,
where we will learn to be civilized ourselves,
through ballroom dance,
of all things,
marking the first time social studies will actually be
social.
But Spanish looks like English—
only better,
more civilized,
with beautiful little arty swirls and marks that do you
the favor of
accenting the important part of a word,
making it seem festive,
fun,
to say
¡Buenos días!

when *Good morning* always sounds very grumpy and
very sleepy
to me
when I wander into the kitchen,
when I
stare
into my cereal,
wishing for accents and art
and sleep.

Pioneers

I was the leader of my wagon train in fifth grade,
braving the elements with my supplies, my team,
my good sense.
It was an imagination assignment, a game we played
laughing loud—
hardy har har—
when some
imaginary person cut his
imaginary hand off with an imaginary ax,
because it was so horrifying
and fake and we were in fifth grade and most
everything is funny
in fifth grade.
But this!
Sixth grade is a real expedition.

My wagon train is a bus I ride with James,
a bus, when I have only ever had my two feet to
carry me,
because I used to be a walker,
just a couple stretches of sidewalk between my house
and Salem Ridge Elementary.
I could practically
stretch out
my arms from my street
and touch it.
Could count on my one and only classroom teacher,
when now I can count on nothing
except not knowing where I'm going
or which teacher—one for each subject—
will be mean,
will be nice,
will be something else new.
Can't count on seeing my Salem Ridge friends either.
Just maybe catching a glimpse of them in the
hallway or in gym class, some of them in my actual
classes—
annoying Jackson in social studies,
Fiona of first-friend fame

in Spanish,
Quinn at lunch,
Lilly (with two *l*'s) in absolutely nothing with me,
out there roaming these
wide and lonesome halls
on her own.
Lonesome is the word.
At the end of a long day where I hardly speak,
except to ask Mr. Kaye for the math sheet because
he skipped me by accident.
I realize he did not see me, because
I am invisible.
Sixth graders are invisible,
heading out each day,
our provisions strapped onto our backs,
heavy with books and snacks,
three-ring binders.
The elements torturing us—
the breath of thirteen-year-olds
pushing back against us,
the spraying spit of an eighth grader ricocheting off
the floor
and onto my arm.

I tread lightly
in these hallways,
I may be no leader here,
where the earth is sticky with sports drink,
but I have instincts still—
I feel a pit in my stomach,
in knots from a hard-to-digest lunch period,
that we may not all survive intact.
We are invisible and exposed
all at once.

Taking Turns

We are supposed to find world peace, or something
like that,
in this dance exercise—
but I cannot even find my partner's eyes,
because my partner,
in a
turn of events—
the worst
in middle school history—
turns out to be Jackson Allen,
one of the famous FOUR ANNOYING BOYS,
son of ANNOYING,
leg-warmer-wearing,
divorced-spiritual-healing-new-best-friend-of-Mom
Jasmine Allen.

Because all the Allens have *J*s to start their names,
which seems like it makes them special
but, as it
turns out,
didn't do anyone any favors, since Jasmine and Jeff are
divorced, which
turned one whole family into two,
just like a regular old family with mismatched initials.
I turn my eyes toward my feet and study them instead
of trying to
turn away from Jackson, and because I have to work
on my footwork.
There is no
turnout
in ballroom dancing, like in ballet,
which I gave up because Fiona and Sara,
my old dancing partners,
had
given up on me.
Just
turning, in general, in ballroom,
while feeling each other's shoulder blades
under our fingertips,

each other's breath,
as we go,
his hands,
JACKSON ALLEN'S HAND,
on my waist.
If you can make peace with your partner,
says Ms. Perez,
knowing somehow that we are
at war,
you can make magic.
If that
turns out to be true,
I think,
I will use my magic to
turn this partner
into a better one.

Home Economics

I fish a check out of my pocket
and hand it to Bonnie,
my piano teacher.
The check has an angry look to it,
I noticed when my dad shoved it into my hand last
night,
at our night at his house.
Their house,
now that he and Stephanie,
who is an art teacher,
are a *they*.
Now that he and Stephanie,
who smells like perfume and spearmint Tic Tacs
all day long,
are going to be a family.

Husband and wife.

An extra mom, Stephanie likes to say,

ha-ha-ing at me,

nervously,

with her spearminty breath.

The writing on the check isn't calm like Mom's.

It's a doctor thing,

James told me

impatiently

last night,

when I showed him.

Don't cry about it, he said,

because the main thing he says to me nowadays is

don't cry about it.

But I know angry when I see it.

What if I told you it costs the

average family

two hundred dollars a week at the grocery store?

This is what Mr. De Marzo asks us in

FACS,

a jaunty abbreviation for

Family and Consumer Sciences,

which is a very serious,

and not jaunty,
subject.
FACS is a class where the word
average
gets tossed around a lot,
and where salads also get tossed because we learn to
cook
an average supper too.
I think about what Mr. De Marzo says, because I
know everything
costs more than I think,
and I wish all the time that everything cost less,
that grocery shopping with Mom
would not feel especially hard.
And I wish piano lessons were free,
actually,
so I could just walk over to Bonnie's house and play
"Monkey on a Carousel"
jauntily,
like the music says.
And I wish that when Mr. De Marzo said
average family,
he meant mine.

Art

A little news.
Mr. Marks is my kind of English teacher,
thinks that how we express ourselves matters,
thinks grammar and the parts of speech are important
too,
says the way we structure our essays and formulate our
thoughts should be artful,
should draw a picture of the idea we are trying to
communicate—
thinks journalism is a good place to start,
to study, to analyze,
to learn how to use
broad brushstrokes and
fine lines
to

paint the portrait of an argument.
The way he speaks
makes me think of writing and reading
as art class,
inspires me to want to read the newspaper
and draw conclusions that will inspire him too.
I wish I could find an artful way to share my news
with Quinn,
to tell her that Jackson Allen is my dance partner,
to ask her if her teacher is making them dance too,
find out if she has to hold hands and make eye contact
with a boy when we both have made an effort to avoid
all contact with all boys
up until now.
I wish I could find some
splashy way to describe what it is like to have
Jackson Allen in my life so much now,
to have him as my mom's best friend's son.
A bold font, perhaps, with exclamation points and
maybe ellipses . . .
for mystery.
If only I could nail her down for a lunchtime
interview,

over chocolate milk and a turkey sandwich.
If only I could find a way to make her read me,
like she used to,
we might connect again,
but the long table has something I do not:
better stories,
better body language,
or better writers, anyway.

How to Dance

Step one: Introduce yourself to your partner.
Step two: Do not murder your partner for being
Jackson Allen.
Step three: Avoid all eye contact, making sure not to
look directly at the evil inside him.
Step four: Smile.
I excuse myself and talk to my social studies teacher,
who seems happy—
very—
about this assignment,
this BALLROOM DANCE unit that has
NOTHING to do with school or civilization
or world peace and should be
OPTIONAL.
I do not think this is for me,

I say.

Oh, but it is, she says, smiling.

Jackson and I don't get along, I want to say.

We are NOT FRIENDS! I want to shout in her
smiling face.

HE CALLED ME MEDUSA IN FOURTH GRADE,
she must know.

Don't be rude, she says.

Your partner is waiting, she says,

and there he is,

staring at me with his hands in the air like he doesn't

mind any of this at all,

making me look bad,

like I am the one who called HIM Medusa,

making HIM feel ugly and small and mad.

I return to my spot,

my cheeks hot, my feet

cold.

Step five: Turn to stone.

Westward Expansion

Come sit by us, she says,
her long black hair
pin straight and shiny
and
longer even
on second glance,
her skin brown, her cheeks rosy,
her eyes bright.
She's the prettiest person I've ever seen.
She is asking Quinn to *sit by us.*
Quinn and not me,
because Quinn is shiny too.
Go ahead, I say, because I really do want her to and
not because
I *don't* want her to.

I do not want her to have to choose,
because that would be awful for me.
GO AHEAD, I say, using my hip to push her along.
Try new things, I say.
I walk away and don't look back, because I don't want
to see Quinn sitting with all those
bright, shiny girls.
I sit with some girl I know from homeroom.
She pats the seat next to her, but I sit across from her
instead,
my back facing the table where Quinn left me
behind.
I look at my new homeroom friend,
my lunch buddy.
Not shiny except for the creases around her nose.
But new.
I'm trying too.

Face Time

Quinn's number appears and I feel my face
light up brighter than
the face of my phone.
What? James says, noticing my face and not the
silent ring, because we have a silent-ring rule between
us because James is so testy these days about noises he
doesn't make himself.
Someone besides you gets calls, Mr. Popularity, I say,
and he rolls his eyes at me because James IS popular
but wears his hair
blue to prove he isn't the kind of
popular that makes kids
popular in movies.
He's the cool guy who usually only becomes
popular at the end of movies.

I understand this about him because these are my
favorite movies, and he
secretly loves this about me, that I
secretly
understand that the
blue of his hair
is meaningful,
that I observe the silent-ring rule,
that I follow his rules in general, except this one
hi-ee! I exclaim at Quinn's freckled face,
not playing it cool, like James,
not acting like I don't care, like James.
Those are his rules and they do not apply to a person
like Quinn, who needs to be greeted properly when
she rings, her smile greeting me properly in return.
How was lunch? I ask.
Why didn't you sit with us? she asks, because we are
straightforward with each other,
except,
I felt bad for some girl, I lie
(because I think that girl felt bad for me),
playing it cool, like James,
except without the blue hair,

just the regular hair of a girl whose best friend is
looking at something else on the screen,
some other incoming information,
something more interesting than me, I can tell from
the dinging and vibrating of her eyes and her phone,
the way her eyes smile and
zigzag across the screen,
pretending to look at me, but pausing
our friendship
to look at something else.
Sit with us tomorrow, Iz, I want her to say, but instead
she says
Who'd ya sit with? Which girl?, not caring about the
answer.
And it feels final.
Feels like we might not sit together tomorrow either,
or maybe ever.
The girl from homeroom, I say, and then I say
I wonder who Lilly's been sitting with,
because I want to change the subject,
play it cool, thinking if my hair were blue, this would
be easier to play off,

thinking my hair is too straightforward for this
conversation.

Some girl named Ginger, Quinn says, always knowing
things about things.

Lilly seems a little weird to me all of a sudden, she says
after that,

her attention still elsewhere.

She was always weird, I say.

So are we, I say.

Right, she says, but I think weird isn't what Quinn
wants to be in middle school,

her eyes darting all around,

a flash of blue hair appearing behind me.

Hi, James! Quinn says, catching a glimpse too,

flirting with my big brother the way I flirt with her

big sister, her dad, who comes home in time for supper

every single night—

each of us wanting what we do not have.

Play it cool, Quinn Mitchell, I say, and we all laugh,

even James.

Holes

The bright and shiny new girl from the long table at
lunch is Heidi,
I learn when my old friend Fiona shouted her name
desperately
in the hall today.
Heidi turned around to Fiona,
I noticed, but didn't look happy to see her.
She looked serious, this Heidi,
flipping her hair the way some of these middle school
girls do,
and making it seem like she had
more important things to do than turn around for
an
overly friendly
Fiona.
I think of the Heidi in the old book Mom used to

read me about a little girl who lives in a mountain
cabin with her grandfather and who finds a way
to open his
closed-up heart,
finds a way to tap into our hearts in the movie version
too,
in wooden clogs and with a dimply smile.
Mountain Heidi even helps a princessy girl in a
wheelchair.
Mountain Heidi is a helper.
This Heidi doesn't appear to be sweet like mountain
Heidi,
or funny,
or Swiss.
That Heidi is fiction, I know,
but this Heidi is
something else.
A girl whose
ripped jeans make my
intact jeans feel
overdressed,
babyish.
But Fiona and Sara just see the smile and the holes
in her jeans.

Fiona and Sara,
my old best friends, my first friends,
the two people I've known the longest,
besides James, who,
if I lived with him alone in a cabin in the mountains
of Switzerland,
it would be A-OK
with me.
Because he would bring the Beatles to listen to,
and he would play practical jokes on me, and I would
make us pasta and eggs,
like I do on Mom's late nights,
and whatever it is in his life here that makes him slam
his door,
and grunt at me,
and snap at Mom,
and roll his eyes at Dad,
whatever that thing is would not follow us up into the
Swiss mountains,
and I would be sweet and funny, and I would find
a hole
and worm my way in,
to open back up
James's closed-up heart.

Current Events

News flash! Dad hates the ballroom dance unit!
Thinks social studies should focus more on studies,
less on social!
Thinks we are too civilized already!
This just in!
Stephanie disagrees.
Stephanie thinks ballroom dance as social studies is
very cool!
Stephanie goes on to grab Dad's hand and pull him
out of his chair and into her arms!
Are you getting this? Can I get a cameraman?
Stephanie makes Dad spin her around the kitchen to
the tune of "Hit the Road Jack,"
a swing number!
Breaking news!

James, new to the ballroom-dance-as-social-studies
conversation, says this is
old news, says they've been trying this dancing unit
for years,
says it stank then and it stinks worse now.
Some might say James is pandering to Dad, agreeing
with him to get some
positive attention
for once.
In an editorial piece, Izzy Kline weighs in:
I don't know what to think, she says. *Dance doesn't seem so
civilized to me, if you think about how you might end up
stepping on someone's toes all the time.*
On the other hand,
Kline continues,
*there is something nice about watching
Dad and Stephanie hit the tile floor
in time with the music.*
It kind of fits their current mood.
*They are the lovebirds on top of the cake that will be
served at their spring wedding,*
*an important current event coming up at the end of this
school year—*

where eye contact will have to be made,
or not made,
in order to
keep the peace
on the dance floor,
and elsewhere in the family.
Only time will tell
which way this will swing.
Back to you.

Homework

I unlock the side door and wonder for the millionth
time
why James wasn't on the bus,
why he didn't feel the need to tell me he was not going
to be on the bus when he knows I do not like—
that I HATE—
to walk into an empty house, where I turn on the TV
immediately to
fill up the quiet space with some noise,
the all-news channel still on from early this morning
when Mom was getting ready
for work,
and I think of
all the work I have to do—math and Spanish and
science and social studies—

flipping the channel on the TV to something that
takes
less work to listen to—
a show with kids who have a cook and a nanny,
who helps them
work out their problems and helps them with
homework too.
A car door slams, and soon the side door slams too.
Got a ride, James says, shaking his head at my TV
selection.
Could have told me, I say.
Could have gotten me a ride too, I think,
like a TV big brother would have, I think. Big
brothers on TV always do the right thing,
always stick up for the little sister at school,
saying things like
you got another thing coming,
then Little Sis kicks the kid in the shins for good
measure and Big Brother pats her on the head and
their
work is done.
I look at the TV screen and not at James because
everything

works out nice like that at the end of a TV show,
by the last commercial break,
because everyone eventually comes home—
both parents, all the siblings, the nanny, the cook—
and because they have some extra time to fill while
the credits roll,
they sit around laughing at it all—
a hard half hour's work done until next time.
James is my only nanny and sometime cook,
an unreliable head-patter,
unlikely to stick up for me, since he wouldn't know
that I need any
sticking up for in the first place.
I stick up for him instead, when Dad says
where's James? when he calls, but James doesn't want
to talk or never came home that day,
well, I say
he's indisposed and I pretend there is a laugh track and
that James is in a funny position that Dad can't see,
but the audience can.
Maybe I pretend that he's upside down
or that his feet are
stuck to the kitchen floor, because things like that
happen on TV and

TV makes sticky situations funny and all of this takes
some
working out, but that's okay.
I am
stuck with James
for more than a half hour at a time—
we have lots of time to
work it all out.

The Writing on the Wall

When you want to hide
from your Spanish lesson
because it is a geography lesson in disguise and
you do not CARE that Puerto Rico is in the
Caribbean,
that Chile is on the Pacific,
Uruguay on the Atlantic.
When you find all these things
not very interesting, and when you keep mixing up
San Juan with San Jose
anyway,
which are apparently vacation spots
for people who don't visit their grandmas in Florida
once a year.

When this happens, YOUR vacation spot becomes
the stall in the girls' bathroom
down the hall from Señora Navalón's classroom.
Where you can rest a minute
from all the exclamation points and accents,
from all the enthusiasm,
and just
read
because there is poetry on the walls.
Poetry, scrawled in different colors,
some things crossed out,
some written in pen or Sharpie or some other forever
ink,
and I wonder who is
so brave to write poetry here.
Roses are red
Violets are blue
Nancy has a face
that belongs in a zoo.
I wonder if *Nancy* knows, or if she ever knew—since
both the poem
and the name feel
old, things from a long time ago,

captured here in this locked-in space,
this smelly time capsule—
that she was so popular and
looked after,
that someone,
a poet,
wrote about her in permanent marker
just down the hall from
¡La clase de la Señora Navalón!
I read it over and over again and think of San Juan
and picture
a beautiful girl named Nancy
on a beach in Puerto Rico.
I want to draw a little palm tree near the poem
for ambience,
but I have no Sharpie,
just my finger
leaving an imaginary
mark.
Nothing too permanent.

Driver's Ed

James and I are home alone because Mom has a late
night at work and because school is
in full swing,
as she says. We are
well into October,
she sighs cheerfully, because she loves October and its
changing leaves
and the fact that there are so many full school days to
be had in October.
But these days feel bumpy to me still,
the road rocky like the ice cream,
marshmallows for speed bumps,
nuts for gravel.
Not a lot of smooth surfaces in middle school.
So many roadblocks,

so much work to do,
so many subjects to cover.
Math, science, English, Spanish.
Lunch,
which I mention out of one corner of my mouth,
the other corner of my mouth chewing the egg
sandwich James made me
while I yelled at him that the gas flame was too high
on the stove,
and while he yelled back
I'M driving this bus, Iz, like he always does.
I am the passenger, he is the driver,
NAVIGATING, I suppose,
while setting things on fire,
I think but do not say.
Lunch is not a subject, James says,
moving one of his big headphones
off his ear, to show me he cares,
to help me
navigate this road he has been down before.
Only James skidded through lunch, probably, with no
trouble, no bumps,
because James's bad behavior makes him

magnetic to all people at all tables in any room at any
time,
and James only ever
veered off the road in math and English, crossing the
actual line in Spanish because HE CHEATED ON A
TEST
and they,
she,
caught him and sirens went off in this house
and Dad was mad and Mom was mad at Dad
for being mad
and I was mad at James for being
SUCH A BAD DRIVER.
He didn't need Dad's yelling and neither did I.
He needed a CRASH course in middle school and in
life and in
cooking eggs on a too-hot stove top.
I should be managing the heat now that James has
failed.
I know when to turn it down,
I am excellent at finding ways to slow down,
turn off at the rest stops,
and refuel.

This is the subject of my thoughts
when James slides that chunky headphone off his
pierced-up ear—
when he tries to tell me what is and
is not a subject—
lunch IS a subject, James.
It is the subject of my biggest fears,
and my biggest road test
yet.
Out of my way.

Vocabulary

Wow, did she have a growth spurt
or what?!
Would you look at her!
What size shoe?
Can you guys share shoes now?
And
Oh, what a figure!
Phew!
The definition of *spurt,*
as I understand it
from a fifth-grade vocabulary unit,
is *to gush forth.*
Maybe I have grown,
taller,
thicker,

longer in the foot,

and maybe the nose too.

And maybe it is all this GROWING that is making

me tired.

Or maybe I am tired also of Mom's friends,

who are always gushing

forth.

Maybe I am EXHAUSTED from that.

Maybe I have some questions for YOU,

when we run into YOU at the drugstore,

and there are people all around,

and you are NOT IN THE MOOD but know to

smile anyway, because

smile, honey, you don't want to look

DISENGAGED,

you want to seem

CHEERFUL.

And maybe I'll say—a little louder than I would

normally talk

about someone else's body,

someone else's

FEET—

maybe I'll say

wow, would you look at that?
What shoe size are YOU?
Are you getting WIDER?
WRINKLIER?
Go FIGURE.
Phew!
Because maybe I am growing at a
perfectly regular pace,
and they are the ones
having the spurt.

Two-Hand Touch

The only good thing about Jackson is his little
brother, Jesse,
who just last year was a
teeny, tiny kindergartner,
which made him one of the little buddies to us
big, important fifth graders—
one of the best parts of being a fifth grader,
besides EVERYTHING,
was having a kindergarten buddy.
My buddy was Tiana, whose brown eyes smiled
at me
when I would read *Harold and the Purple Crayon*
to her,
who reached for my hand in the hall when I would
pass by,

who made me a
birthday card
and whose mom was
touched
when I made Tiana one too.
We have to stop by Jesse's peewee
football game because Mom wants to say
a quick *hi-ee*
to her best friend, Jasmine,
and it is so cold for a fall day,
so chilly, that when I
touch the car door,
it stings my fingers a little,
and they are still stinging when
we sit down on the blanket
with Jasmine and Jackson.
I don't look at Jackson's eyes and I am thankful
he doesn't look at mine.
I smile at Jasmine the way Heidi
fake smiles at Fiona and Sara,
but Jasmine,
I think,
is onto me.

You came! I'm
touched!
Jesse will be
touched too, Izzy, she says.
Never mind Jackson,
who sneers because Jackson is
touchy,
after all.
Always was.
Jesse Allen, though, is different.
Like Tiana, he would reach out to me too,
touching my hand in the hall,
touching my heart a little because sometimes
he reached out for Tiana's hand too,
when she cried because kindergarten can be hard for a
little buddy
who is missing
her mom,
who is insisting
she wants to go
home,
who would draw her way there
if only she had Harold's purple crayon,

but who only has regular crayons,
and the magic
touch
of a fifth grader named Izzy Kline.

Dress-Up

Lilly comes over to play, while all the other girls in the
world seem to be playing something else,
soccer or dance or
on their phones.
Who do you sit with at lunch? I ask her while I sit on
my bed and she rummages through my closet.
Wherever, she says, her voice muffled from some
situation she has gotten herself into. Lilly has been
getting herself into situations forever, so I know
from the sound of her voice,
from the muted screech,
that this is the case.
I open the closet door and find her butt up in the air,
her head buried in a deep sea of old costumes.
She is stuck inside my old dress-up box.

She has thrown herself in, as she does.

She is silent, laughing so hard I cannot hear her, and I
feel my insides start to explode and I laugh too.

Help! she screams, and I scream too, a laughing,
cackling scream, and try pulling her out by the feet,
and then we are on top of each other, laughing so
hard my stomach hurts, tears dripping out of my eyes.

I might even be drooling.

Lilly fixes herself and stands up and gets back to the
matter at hand.

I calm down too but kind of want to laugh that way
again, and right away, because I realize I haven't
laughed

in weeks.

Months?

Let's dress up, Lilly says, and I want to hate the idea
but I love it instead.

It is an eighty-degree day in October,

fall dressing up like summer,

so we wear bathing suits and sunglasses and make
some snacks,

Ritz crackers with peanut butter and

Marshmallow Fluff and

club sodas with a lemon twist, and
we lay out a picnic blanket in the backyard,
and we lay ourselves down on it, the grass
stiff and itchy underneath us,
and we
look up at the fall colors,
knowing we won't be able to pretend like this for
much longer.
Lilly hums in her weird Lilly way, moving all around
because she
can't sit still, and she goes inside and comes back out
with
some dolls
and a sun hat and she looks like a glamorous mom,
propping up her babies for a nice day in the park,
sipping tea out of some pretend cup she found
at the bottom of that bin.
She's so comfortable dressing up and being herself at
once.
Ask me questions, she says.
Start a conversation, she begs.
Pretend I am your mom friend!
Why can't I go sit with those girls at lunch? I think.

Why don't I just sit wherever I want?
Why do they make me feel
stiff and itchy from underneath?
Where do I even want to sit?
Why can't I play the part and be myself
all at once?
I look at Lilly and wonder how she got to be so funny,
wonder also if Quinn is having half this much fun
wherever she is,
wonder why she couldn't come over today,
hoping she didn't have something better to do.
Go ahead, ask me! Lilly says.
Sure is nice to get an extended summer, I say,
pretending. *How long do you think this will last?*
Oh, who knows?! Lilly says, with a lot of drama in her
voice.
Let's just enjoy it while it lasts.
Then she clinks her teacup with mine, flips over,
sticks her butt in my face, and says
bottoms up!
and we crack up all over again.

Trick or Treat

What if you were so excited for Halloween that you
ate a whole bowl of Halloween candy while watching
a scary Halloween movie and then
you couldn't sleep because the movie scared you
AWAKE and
what if you couldn't decide if you should be a football
player because you may as well since you have a jersey
already
because James is a football fan
or what if you were to be a cheerleader or a creepy doll,
or a creepy cheerleader,
or an old lady because you have that cane from Mom's
work
or *oooh!* what if you were a zombie on crutches
because you have the crutches from the time you
thought you

rolled your ankle when you and Quinn and Lilly tried
out James's skateboard,
and you went flying down the driveway and almost
peed in your pants when you fell and Dad brought
home
those crutches from the office even though he
rolled his eyes at you in front of everyone at dinner
that night at his house.
And what if you didn't fall asleep until four in the
morning and then
woke up and realized that
every single other person you know is going as
a group something-or-other
and you don't have any plans at all other than to meet
up with Lilly
and maybe Quinn.
Maybe but probably not, because she's part of
something else—
a big group of referees to all the boys who are football
players—
which means you can't really be a football player after all
because that would be weird, since you weren't
technically INVITED to be a referee and since you
are not a boy.

And what if now you realize you can't be a cheerleader
or even a creepy cheerleader because you don't want it
to look like you are
trying to fit into
the group costume somehow,
and now the only option really IS a toilet-papered-up
zombie because you want to
cover yourself up entirely
because you were
up all night and
you are exhausted and also
you are nervous and
it is cold outside and
you need to
PROTECT yourself
from the living.
What if.

Parade

There was a time when we circled the pavement on
the school playground and stopped and smiled for
pictures,
hugged each other tight,
cheek to cheek,
smearing princess makeup all over someone else's
mermaid face,
me clip-clopping along in the wooden shoes my
parents had brought me from Switzerland,
parading around as a Heidi type,
a little Dutch girl.
It will be so authentic! my mom had said, giddy.
Me pretending not to be in horrible pain,
the wooden edges of my authentic shoes
piercing the skin of my heels with each

clip and clop.
Looking up ahead toward my brother,
big-time fifth grader,
clowning around with his big-time friends,
Mom waving at us, still giddy.
That was so long ago, it seems impossible.
See ya, kiddos, Jasmine says now to Jackson and me as
the two of them
wave the two of us off into town, where we will
parade around,
separately, but near each other—
referees chasing down the football players and not for
fouls, not for warnings,
just for the game of it,
and Jackson says
Mommy, stop! and I
stop in my zombie tracks because
Jackson just called his mom
Mommy,
and it is sweet and spicy like that packet of
Hot Tamales I just ate,
and then I am on fire, because Jackson is maybe
sweet and spicy too, which makes me so nervous

I snap,
snorting through my toilet-papered face,
and Jasmine snaps too,
a picture of us,
me snorting,
Jackson rolling his eyes, with thick black swipes
underneath to protect him from
my glare later on, when
Jackson and his boys are busy clowning around,
and girls in big groups are busy
parading around with Heidi and her type,
and me, clip-clopping still,
trying to catch up to them,
still looking up ahead to the big time.

Waltz

I am stiff as a board, my arms up high and poised to perfect
the dance at hand.
Relax, people, says Ms. Perez, my social studies teacher,
who continues to school us in ballroom dance as a
study in communication and civilized behavior.
This is not a waltz, people, she says, eyeing Jackson and
me specifically,
and I think of Jackson saying *Mommy* and I soften
my stance.
He softens too, and we go on like this,
back and forth until we are almost on the floor,
my arms turning to spaghetti as Jackson tries harder
and harder to be a proper partner,
faking a man face,

and I laugh the kind of laugh that comes out silent
and then turns into hiccups.
We fall into a pool of each other's silliness.
This is the SAMBA! sings Ms. Perez, and she
snaps her fingers
and we snap to attention,
standing up again,
holding ourselves
together again.
Jackson snaps his fingers and flips his hip to one side,
and we dance,
and as we go, Jackson counts with a fake Spanish
accent that starts out a little ridiculous but ends up
flat-out funny and I snort because
lately I am always SNORTING around him,
and I lose my posture again,
doubling over again,
and he drags me along and we are doing something in
the same direction,
but not dancing.
I hate you, I mouth,
swallowing a laugh.
I hate you too, he mouths back.

I laugh again, and try not to be mad at him for
making me misbehave when I do really
want to get this right.
Sorry I called you Medusa, he whispers,
and I am so surprised
my face gets hot.
I stand up straight again and
try to quiet down the butterflies that have
waltzed back into my life.
They seem to know this is a samba,
even if I do not.
It's okay, I say.
Maybe *hate* is too strong a word, I think.

Whisper Down the Alley

Lilly heard from Quinn
who heard from Fiona
who heard from Sara
who heard from Jackson
who probably heard it in his group chat
on his mom's old phone—
a chat that is probably not called
but should be called
FOUR ANNOYING BOYS TALKING ON A
GROUP CHAT—
that one of those boys has a crush
on Quinn.
When Lilly asks me if I am upset,
I am confused because the only upsetting part is that

eleven-year-olds are pretending to have crushes as if
they are
teenagers,
when they are little boys playing with their moms'
old toys.
Because what if it is Jackson?
she asks.
What if it is?
I ask back, scrunching up my whole face to SHOW her
IN PERSON
that I have NO IDEA what she is even talking about
right now.
Well, because you hate him,
she says,
but she says it in a way that
sounds like she means that
I like him,
which I do not.
It is just that I no longer MIND him.
I think that if Lilly told Quinn who
told Fiona
and Fiona told Sara
and Sara told Jackson

that I scrunched up my nose at the thought of any of
this,
well, I think Jackson would think that I DO like him,
and not that I just
don't mind him,
don't mind it when he is my dancing partner and
makes me laugh
because he sings the samba song
in pretend Spanish.
Don't mind when I make him laugh back,
when I slouch down so we are the same height for the
tango.
Don't mind when we make eye contact
BECAUSE WE ARE GETTING GRADED ON
EYE CONTACT.
And when we burst into snorts like it is a staring
contest and not a silly dancing project that won't solve
the problem of
world peace.
Anyway, I straighten out my face and shrug instead so
that
Lilly will tell Quinn
who will tell Fiona

who will tell Sara
who will tell Jackson
that I didn't scrunch up my face,
that I shrugged him off,
that he can like Quinn all he wants.
If he even does,
if it isn't one of the other FOUR ANNOYING
BOYS,
which it might be because who knows who will tell
who
what
and when
next.

The Natural World

Poetry is weird
sometimes it must follow rules
five seven five beats

Haiku is like this
we learn in my English class
something Japanese

I like these poems
something to do with nature
sights that surround us

The natural world
is filled with things that we touch
and that touch us too

In this smelly stall
someone wrote on the gray wall
unnaturally

She wrote a poem
about a boy she once liked
who liked someone else

It's a limerick
limericks can be funny
but sometimes racy

I look away now
I prefer haiku poems
they are quiet, sweet

I would write one here
in this unnatural place
in pencil only

It could be erased
would need to be wiped away
they could never know

It would go like this
a crush on her enemy
what if he found out

An observation
this crush this feeling this thought
is not natural

History

A long, long time ago,
in the olden days
of elementary school,
you wouldn't necessarily know
who was doing what
with whom
and when.
You might happen to hear,
by messenger or by
gossip,
that so-and-so
and
so-and-so
went to see that movie together,
maybe with their families because their families are
friends.

Or maybe that other so-and-so
and
so-and-so
went to the mall,
like in fourth grade when the so-and-sos happened
to be
Fiona and Sara,
my old best friends,
who happened to wear the
exact same thing to
Polar Express day at school,
a warm and fuzzy Christmas-spirit-type day when
everyone wore pajamas
and when no one cared whether or not Christmas was
your holiday.
(It wasn't.)
And they had obviously planned to wear the exact
same pajamas,
but I didn't
KNOW THAT FOR A FACT.
Nowadays,
we find things out
by other methods,

by pictures,
by typed messages
too,
FACTUAL INFORMATION transferred from
person to person
in ways that make our palms light up,
and our insides
light up too
when the news is good,
when someone wants to sit next to you on the bus on
the way home.
But which feels like a punch in your formerly lit-up
stomach
when Quinn Mitchell, who you thought was your
friend forever,
who was president of the no-friend club you created
together
when you were almost ten and
almost
friendless—
BFF 4 EVAH, you wrote in each other's yearbooks in
fifth grade—
tells you that she cannot sit with you on the bus,

cannot come over after school because of a doctor
appointment,
and when you believe her because there was a time in
her life
when she had cancer,
CANCER,
which she survived
to become the best friend you have ever had,
so you believe her every word—
until the punch in the gut that might send YOU
to the doctor instead,
until you see her
pictured,
smiling,
along with
TYPED-UP MESSAGES,
with girls who aren't you,
girls named Heidi and other things,
that very afternoon,
shopping for things they will maybe wear together
one warm and fuzzy day, celebrating something that
doesn't belong to you,
and which everyone

in history
now knows
for certain,
4 EVAH,
for a fact.

Honor System

I no longer have to log my reading, just have to read
as much as I can each day,
because my English teacher trusts us,
says he believes we want to read,
want to get involved with a good book,
thinks it will offer us
an escape.
Gonna read tonight? he asks us as a group at the end
of each English period, and each of us has to reply,
individually,
on my honor.
I pick up *Yours Till Niagara Falls, Abby* and
escape back to camp, where Quinn sent the book in
the first place,

where she thought to pack it up and write my name in bubble letters on a puffy envelope and my address too and

put stickers on it too.

Back when nothing new had happened yet,

when my biggest problem was finding a way to get out of cleaning the toilets,

since it was my turn, according to the chore wheel.

Feeling nostalgic? Mom asks, standing at my door.

I look up at her and even though I see her almost every day,

I feel like I haven't seen her in a while.

I pat the bed and she bounces up and down in a funny way on purpose to make the bed shake and I think she seems

bouncier in general than she has in a while.

That book gives me flashbacks of camp, Mom says.

Flashbacks? I ask.

It's an oldie, she says.

Like moi, she says, suddenly French and definitely bouncy.

Good flashbacks or bad ones? I ask, wanting to keep her here forever.

Both, she says, *flashbacks are usually both.*

There were good days and bad days back then just like
there are now.
Feels like a lot of bad days, I say, trying not to cry,
trying not to take
the bounce out of the conversation.
Tell me, she says.
I shake my head.
Keep talking about camp, I say, *about something else.*
Hmmm, she says,
hang on, she says, and she runs out of my room. I get
cozy and brace myself for her return, because when
she does,
I know it will be worth the wait.
She runs back in and leaps onto my bed and leans
over me to turn out my light
and she hands me a flashlight
and I can feel her energy
and we look up to the ceiling, pointing our flashlights
at the darkness,
and she says
I remember playing flashlight tag on the ceiling of my
bunk with my friends,
and then she makes her flashlight tag mine and I
make my flashlight run away,

and I laugh because this game is so silly,
and she says *and I remember not being able to sleep*
when everyone else was sleeping
and *I remember the camp carnival when my friends and*
I dressed up like hippies and this cute boy asked me to
marry him in the marriage booth and made me a ring
out of tinfoil and I was so happy until he married my
best friend next.
No way, I say.
Way, she says.
People can be terrible right after they're wonderful, and
they can be wonderful right after they're terrible. Once
you figure that out, life gets easier, she says.
Hmmm, I say.
Promise you'll talk to me whenever you need? she asks.
On my honor, I say.
Then I get back to chasing her on the ceiling and
think that
this right now
is a flashback
in the making.

Light Reading

At camp I had a night-
light
(not a flashlight)
that clipped onto my summer reads—
light things
like *Betty and Veronica* comics and
the old-timey book Quinn sent me in a package, called
Yours Till Niagara Falls, Abby, which is funny and says
everything in the world anyone needs to know about
Quinn Mitchell—that she is charming
and
lighthearted,
and sends unusual camp packages.
I also got a
heavy stack of magazines from Mom

with how-to articles, things
every girl should know,
things *you don't wanna miss . . .*
or else,
and I flipped through them once or twice but put
them aside, since something about them was
weighing me down.
I tossed them into the trash when we packed up,
saving only one article,
a bubbly page with big letters that said
"The Only Tween Makeup Workbook You'll Ever
Need,"
complete with tips, and blank spaces,
makeup goals,
which I folded into the shape of a bookmark
and tucked into the book Quinn had sent.
I thought we'd study up—
thought we'd cram that torn-out page plus a whole
summer
into a big reunion hug in front of Carvel,
thought we'd have time before before summer
officially thinned out into fall,
before we were in the thick of things—

to devise a plan to avoid cosmetic
and other pitfalls.
Thought we'd have time before
middle school called,
before Niagara
falls.

Flashback

We are loaded up with shopping bags of
sharpened pencils
and
lined loose-leaf paper—two packs—
and
either a roll of paper towels or a box of tissues
and
about one million other things that weigh a lot,
but Mom gets caught up outside,
talking to other grown-ups about the
ridiculous heat wave,
and the fact that there is
NO AIR-CONDITIONING
and
it was such a nice summer and now this, just in time
for the first day of school

and what will they do?

And I am impatient to see everyone.

It isn't the real first day.

It is drop-your-supplies-and-meet-your-teacher-and-see-
all-your-friends-and-old-teachers day,

the day before

the first day.

The day that supplies you

with all you need to know about the first day—

who is at your table,

what your classroom smells like, and

if your teacher is nice.

School supplies.

Quinn is at my table, and Fiona and Sara.

My new best friend and my old best friends all in one place,

making me sweatier,

if that's even possible.

It is hotter inside than out but it smells like school and
erasers and Quinn,

who taps me on the shoulder and we jump up

and down because I was away and then she was away

and it has been so long,

but just like that,

I forget summer.

Until the ice cream truck rolls up outside,
supplying us with cones and sprinkles and a
last-ditch effort
at summer.
We sit on the curb of the school,
with the grown-ups talking,
and our hands free of the
heavy baggage we came in with,
ice cream dripping between our fingers.
Summer it is—
for a little while longer,
long enough to finish up our ice cream
and baby-wipe our hands,
and be our old fourth-grade selves for
one last lick.
I shake off the memory,
my eyes stinging with tears.
I am still in middle school,
no ice cream dripping down my wrists,
no last licks.
Just firsts
and firsts
and firsts.

Thanksgiving

I am thankful
for getting an A- on my Spanish test,
for James's taste in music,
for Mom's garlic smashed potatoes,
for Dad's convertible,
for Lilly's extra *l*—
For my children, Mom interrupts,
for yoga, she also says,
for Jasmine and Jackson and Jesse, she says, and I smile
at the Jesse part,
cringe at the Jasmine and Jackson part—
for you guys, Jasmine says back,
for the dethert, Jesse says
(and I am secretly thankful for his lisp),
and around and around we go

until Mom says
James? and he shrugs and she says
you can say for my charming mom, *you know,*
and he says *for my weird mom* and she seems okay
with that and I am
thankful that weird is okay with her even if it isn't
okay with Quinn anymore,
even if Dad says,
every single Thursday night lately,
that it is weird that Mom is always with *that weirdo
yogi,*
weird that they finish each other's sentences,
and which makes me think how weird that he cares in
the first place,
weird that he found someone to replace Mom so fast,
weird that he can't be happy that Mom is not alone
and crying as much anymore,
which makes me think that
one person's weird is another person's wonderful,
and I am grateful for that too,
grateful that everyone has lots to be thankful for,
and that around and around we go.

Tango

Quinn pops her head into my social studies lesson
today,
walks in to grab a notebook she left behind and
I let go of Jackson's hand,
which I am clutching in the first place ONLY because
we are having a dance lesson where we have to be
closer than usual,
cheek to flushed
cheek.
Having to come
face to flushed
face with Quinn now for the first time in a while,
I turn away but Jackson does not.
He looks at her in that way people want to be looked
at, and that's when I realize how pretty she has gotten,

how her cheeks are flushed not from dancing with
someone she used to hate
but from maybe just getting here in a hurry,
to grab something she left behind,
to take a minute to notice me,
to notice Jackson,
to note that he is looking at her and I am looking at
him, and she is looking for a missing
notebook.
Okay, people, let's get back to it, Ms. Perez says.
IT TAKES TWO TO TANGO.

Friction

There was a Hanukkah when James and I got flannel
pajamas and flannel sheets from Aunt Liv,
which she insisted we put on our beds
that instant
and which we were both actually pretty excited about.
I might have been five.
James might have been eleven.
My age now.
This year,
Aunt Liv doesn't come to our Hanukkah.
She goes to Dad's Hanukkah.
Liv belongs to him and to us,
but not to Mom,
even though they used to talk late at night about
recipes

and work and
everything else in the world.
Dad picks us up on the second night,
the night after we have latkes and applesauce with
Mom
and Jackson's mom.
And Mom's mom.
Grandma, who came all the way from Florida
to *freeze her rear end off* and beat us at the dreidel
game, and give us some gelt,
shiny silver dollars that feel heavy in my palm and
filled with possibilty.
I hug Mom extra tight because I don't know what
she'll do while we're opening loads of things she might
never see.
Things we'll keep at Dad's
probably.
At the door, falling out of the hug,
I flash back to the flannel sheets and the sparks that
flew when I got under my covers that night—
when James was eleven
and I was five.
Hey, James!

I yelled.
Hey, Izzy!
he yelled back.
Crazy flannel sparks!
Yeah, me too!
And we laughed across the hall and kicked our feet
to make crazy blue sparks fly around in the dark.
Friction
is what my teacher says when we rub our hands
together
to make heat.
Friction
is what Aunt Liv says,
rubbing her hands together,
when I ask why we can't all have Hanukkah
together
for old times' sake.
There were sparks downstairs too, that night,
while we were making a cozy light show
with our pajamas and sheets,
but not blue sparks
and
not exciting sparks

and not flannel sparks
and not
cozy sparks.
But friction sparks,
still.

Each of Us
Is a Flower

Go back to kindergarten, dummy,
says the poet of the second stall of the bathroom
in the gym,
the bathroom where I go when I need a breather
after the pacer test,
after running sprints, sweat pouring out of every part
of my body—
parts of my body I didn't even know I could
sweat out of.
The same bathroom I used back when Dad and Mom
and I would
sit on the bleachers and watch James
sit on the bench
during his basketball games.
Maybe I was in kindergarten.

Maybe whoever wrote this little number was writing
about me or maybe she wrote it just yesterday and
maybe someone had kindergarten-type behavior that
made her so mad she had to write about it on the gym
bathroom wall.

Maybe she forgets that in kindergarten we used to
take little rests,

putting our heads on our cool desks in the dark
because the teacher had turned out the lights and
the outside light would stream in and bounce off the
shiny hair of kindergartners who had probably taken
baths the night before,

moms scrubbing their heads with three-in-one
shampoo,

running the faucet to wash away the soap suds and
the day,

water pouring over their little kindergarten faces,
cleaning everything up.

Maybe she didn't have a teacher who taught them how
to hold hands when someone was upset,

taught her how to read by skipping over the hard
words and

finding meaning in the words that surrounded them.

Maybe she didn't have a teacher who worked all spring
to teach them a show where they would
each sing a different part
and where they would
each have hand motions and where they would
perform,
each one squeaky clean and rested up from all the
kindergarten days spent resting their shiny heads on
their cool desks.
"Each of Us Is a Flower"
was the song, I think now.
Or maybe she *did,* this poet,
and maybe the dummy *does* need to go back to
kindergarten,
needs a little extra help,
another rest period,
another bath,
some more time,
some space too,
to sprout.
I think of Quinn.
She could use a time-out.
Go back to kindergarten, dummy, I whisper.

Cooking

I am supposed to meet Lilly here in this lunchroom
turned ballroom
turned Winter Dance,
this place that smells of meatball sandwiches from
Friday's lunch special,
the kitchen shut down for the night,
parents handing out snacks and bottled water instead,
while everyone bounces, which wouldn't count as
dancing in social studies—
where we have spent so much time learning to stay
grounded in our tango,
feet glued to the floor—
but seems to here, where, instead of
gliding across the classroom floor,
boys slide across the floor

on their knees,

their phones poised above for picture taking.

Nothing else poised, except me,

determined to fit in,

having put on my face—

as my grandma would say—

a little of this and a little of that,

thinking of Mr. De Marzo talking in FACS about

seasoning things

to make a dull recipe more palatable,

mixing it up a bit with my look until I see the girls

from the long table,

huddled together, pointing in my direction,

their looks searing me,

and I feel that I have overseasoned,

maybe let myself marinate too long,

know that I have made myself less palatable,

not more,

that I have to bounce,

as they say,

get out of this cauldron,

somehow,

find a way to skim something off the top at least,

to see if I can rescue this recipe or if I should
just eat it,
make the best of the whole mess and
get down on my knees,
hoist my phone above my head,
and savor this moment for posterity—
hashtag epic fail.

Makeup

I missed it,
never did go back and review,
wasn't paying attention when we got word
that there would be
a test.
I thought I would have more time to study
the material,
more time to think about
all the information—
so much information!—
in the pages of that glossy,
shouting
workbook.
Three SIMPLE steps to a SMOKY EYE!
BEST SMEARS FOR LUSCIOUS LIPS!
JUST-PINCHED CHEEKS FOR ALL!

I could remember only
one of the steps,
in the end.
Forgot to smudge.
Not so simple
after all.
I needed more time to get it right,
to get the perfect score,
my first time out in the world
with makeup—
besides Halloween when I was little,
when Mom put rosy cream blush on my
Little Mermaid cheeks,
for the just-pinched look.
Perfect, for a mermaid.
I got everything wrong,
got whispered about
at the mixer,
which mixed mostly body odor with
not much else.
I failed.
And I'm pretty sure there is
no makeup.

Fairy Tale

I grab a wad of paper towels and wet them and scrub
my face off.
I do not cry,
just scrub.
I should have also read the "How to Give Yourself a
Facial in a Hurry" page.
Shoulda, coulda, woulda.
Then I sit in a stall I have never been in before in a
part of the building where the older kids are,
where I will be next year,
if I even make it to next year.
There is so much to look at here—hearts and flowers
and
eighth-grade graffiti.
Nancy was here.
The girl from my first bathroom poem,

the smelly time capsule.

I hear the door open and Lilly pops her head in.

Iz? echoes into the hollow space, the sink still leaking from my

undoing.

Hi, I say.

You okay? she asks, wetting a towel and handing it to me under the door.

I'm fine, I say. *Just having a little too much fun,* I say.

Ha ha, she says. *Me too,* she says.

You seem fine to me, I say.

Well, isn't that a fairy tale? She laughs and I laugh and shake my head

because Lilly says things like

isn't that a fairy tale and sounds like a person on TV and not like an eleven-year-old girl who happens to be

a character.

My mom says I'm a mess, she says, and she sits down right there on the gross floor

of this

uncivilized place,

on the other side of the stall.

If you're a mess, what am I? I ask, unlatching the stall door and
leaving my old friend Nancy behind.
You're a disaster, she says.
Let's go home. We'll put
cold cream on your face
and ice cream in our mouths
and maybe watch a movie where the weird girls win,
she says,
latching her arm into mine,
and we head outside to meet Lilly's mom, who has
been waiting all night in her car in the parking lot
because she is the type of mom who waits in her car
all night
for a moment just like this,
just in case.
I glance sideways into the gym and see Quinn
and Heidi and all those new girls looking happy and
not noticing us leaving, and it's hard to believe they
aren't all doing fine,
hard to believe that they've shed even one tear,
put on their lip gloss too thick,
laid anything on too thick,

hard to believe Quinn was ever mine, even though I
know that
once upon a time,
she was.

Flashback

Quinn's pinkie hooks onto my pinkie.
We are going in.
We wear what we wore to school that day,
leggings probably,
tank tops,
high-tops.
Buns on
the tops
of our heads.
Twins, basically.
Together, as one,
we disappear from the DJ, who wants us to
GET THE PARTY STARTED!
We stand in the corner and scream at each other
because it is SO LOUD and

we are hoarse the next morning,
when we wake up,
on the floor of Quinn's room
after a sleepover where we talked about
that DJ and that NOISE,
and those girls who had put on lip gloss—
Fiona and Sara!—
for the occasion of our first mixer,
mixing all the schools together,
and shaking us up.
We do not mix,
Quinn and me.
We stick to the sides mostly,
pinkies locked,
and watch everyone else get mixed up, trying to dance
the way people dance at a sixth-grade party,
when we're still only in fifth grade,
jumping,
sweating,
mixing the bounce-house parties from when we were
little
with the bounce of something else
our tank-top bras couldn't quite
keep from bouncing.

Footwork

This is a terrible song, I say.
It's a rumba, Jackson says.
How do you know that? I say,
tired of Jackson knowing everything about everything
all the time.
My dad, he says.
Your dad? I ask. Jackson's dad is a doctor,
like mine.
I picture my own dad in his white coat and his
stethoscope and I think he has never danced the
rumba.
He has never even said the word *rumba,*
I bet.
What kind of doctor is your dad? I ask.
Thinking maybe he's a podiatrist.
Thinking a podiatrist would know something about
the rumba.

Thinking a podiatrist fixes feet, and a lot of feet would
maybe hurt
from dancing the rumba
too much.
He's gone, he says.
That's not a kind of doctor, I say,
trying to be
light,
but Jackson looks down
at his feet.
Our feet.
Left last week, he says.
Where'd he go? I say,
and he looks back up,
but not at my eyes.
Florida, he says, and it sounds like something catches
in his throat,
the way a zipper catches
exactly when you are trying so hard
just to
get going,
to get outside.
I want to say *Florida has airports that play tropical
music when you arrive,*

and beaches and fake ice-skating rinks outside in the
million-degree heat,
and Florida has my beautiful, funny grandma.
I want to tell him we almost always go to Florida over
winter break but not this year because flights are
too damn expensive, but I don't want him to think about
the expense of visiting his dad,
don't want him to have to talk again either before he
can
zip up.
Before we can get back in step
with the rest of the class.
I thought my dad was gone once, I say instead,
thinking of that chilly day.
I was roller-skating in Mom's old-fashioned
roller skates, which I had found in the garage,
mixed up with other old-timey things,
while they talked inside,
the clickety-clack of the thick wheels over the
cracks in the sidewalk,
quieting the sound of someone packing.
It was too cold to be roller-skating.
His leaving us only meant that he would no longer
live with us,

Dad said
after I had exchanged my roller skates for
regular shoes,
and we had
stepped outside
into the cold again.
It also meant he would not ever be there again—
in the middle of the night to shoo the witches out of
my room,
I thought, as we walked around together picking up
fall leaves
for a school project I should have done a week earlier,
before the cold had started to crisp them up—
wouldn't be there to usher those witches out
through the window and back into the black night,
where they belong.
Light on your feet! Ms. Perez says now,
and I think about those leaves and pick up my feet
so I won't crunch them.
Dad had been gone from us for a good, long time
before that
too-cold-for-roller-skating day,
but not now—now he's around more than he ever was,

and anyway, the witches knew to stay away while he
was gone,
and have stayed away since.
He'll be back, I say to Jackson, my heart heavy,
my feet light.
He looks at me in the eyes for maybe the first time
ever,
and I don't look away.

New Year, New You

Hey, how's Quinn, anyway? Mom asks, her mouth
filled with salad because Jasmine tells her pizza is
INFLAMMATORY,
and Mom trusts in Jasmine more than she
trusts in pizza.
Fine, I say, shrugging off her salad eating and her
question
at once.
I don't want to waste time talking about how Quinn
is when we are at Mario's, a pizza place so good you
don't mind that the chairs spin around and make you
dizzy and that the lady who runs the place
chases after unruly teenagers with a wooden spoon.
The spoon lady, James calls her.
James isn't here tonight, though, so I have no one to
joke with.

You didn't tell me about Jackson's dad,
I say back,
my mouth half-full of pizza.
He told you? she asks.
I told him he'd be back, I say. *He'll be back, right?*
He'll be back, she says, then she looks down at her
phone.
It's nice that you two are friends now, she says, and I
hate that she noticed.
Not friends, I say, *dancing partners.*
She doesn't notice that I am being sassy,
that I act sassy when I am embarrassed.
I don't know where James is, she says to her phone like
her phone might answer her back, like this:
*James is on his way and will turn back into your
happy-go-lucky favorite child in
five, four, three, two . . .*
But her phone does not tell her that,
cannot tell her that, because
it isn't possible,
the same way it isn't possible for me to go back to
fourth grade and
hating Jackson Allen, and
loving Quinn Mitchell.

Backward isn't an option unless you are James, right
now walking toward us and wobbling away from us
at once.
The door of Mario's has swung open and the gust of
air is cold but
James is on fire,
his face sweaty, his body swaying, and as he gets closer,
I recognize the smell of alcohol from Mom and Dad's
old New Year's Eve parties—
bottles and sparkling glasses and
sparklier *Happy New Year!* horns
lined up for their guests,
James and me lined up too,
in front of the TV with little cocktail plates of
pigs in blankets and cheese and crackers
and tall plastic flutes filled up with
sparkling apple cider,
ready to party in our pj's on a New Year's Rockin' Eve.
We should have had a sparkly party and
pigs in blankets because Mario's suddenly feels
brightly lit and cold and I feel afraid that James has
slipped just out of my grasp while I was busy with
makeup and dancing and
myself.

Hey, Spoon Lady, he shouts,

waving in a big, weird wave.

James Kline, get your butt over here, Mom says, gritting

her teeth and slamming her phone down on the table,

and it lights up like the crystal ball in Times Square

just at the moment James's eyes

light up and he trips over something

himself.

He falls flat on his face, blood trickling out of the

scar on his chin from when he once flew over the

handlebars of his dirt bike, a long time ago,

before Dad left

and before all of this moodiness and

before he cheated on that Spanish test and

before he cheated me out of a big brother who knows

better than to come to Mario's Pizza

drunk

on New Year's Eve, when the Spoon Lady is on duty.

Knows better than to bring us all down to his

level just when things were looking up

for Mom, at least.

Everyone in the whole place is on his level now,

crowding around him, lying on the floor like that

fallen crystal ball, except me because it was a text that

lit up Mom's phone, and it was just sitting there on
the sticky table,
displaying,
for me to see,
a message from Jasmine Allen,
Happy New Year!
I love you.
My heart stops because I know this isn't a regular-
friend *love you,*
or a text-from-Grandma-in-Florida
love you.
They say be careful what you write in a text.
They say you can't tell meaning over text.
But I can, this time.
This text means love,
and you can't ever go backward from that.

Science

Look up, it's me!
Look down, under your feet,
it's pee!
says the stall wall today,
an experiment
in trying to scare people, I think,
into peeing on the floor,
but I always read ahead, and hardly ever go into the
bathroom to pee anyway.
I am the variable in this experiment, I think,
since, yes, I know that
under my feet is sticky, stinky bathroom tile,
but I know other things.
I know that underneath the tile is probably some
cement,

and underneath that is the earth
that we talk about in the science class I walked out of
to get here,
and underneath that is soil and rocks and
more earth,
and more still beneath that.
Just like underneath all the tequila
and blood from his opened-up scar and also
underneath the throw-up—
because James needed to throw up
to sober up—
was more James than I've seen in a while,
groaning and even crying a little because tequila
doesn't feel as good coming up as it does
going down
apparently.
We had to dig deep, Mom and me,
we had to scratch away at the surface
to get to the bottom of what had happened—
what had made James so mad or
so sad in the first place,
what had made Mom and Dad fall in love,
what had made them fall out of love,

what had made Mom find her way out of back pain
and sadness and discover
a layer of herself she didn't know was there—
through yoga and Jasmine
and the kind of friendship that when you look
underneath it
is true love.
James threw up again after that because I think it is
probably
hard to swallow the fact that your mom has a
girlfriend all of a sudden after a lifetime of boyfriends,
and also because of all that tequila
and because of all the science and all the digging and
what we found.
What starts out sticky and stinky and superficial
sometimes leads you
somewhere deep,
which in this case,
when we got to the bottom
of it all,
was ourselves—
boiled down to our
hot, liquidy core.

Spin the Bottle

Lilly heard from Sara
who heard from Fiona
who heard from Heidi
that Quinn spun the bottle and that the bottle
landed on Jackson and that . . .
What?!
I don't know.
That's all I know.
Because when everyone else is somewhere spinning
something and you are busy spinning and spinning
and spinning and not stopping on anyone
because sometimes things spin
OUT OF CONTROL,
then you miss the controlled
spinning and rely on everyone else spinning
stories you don't really want to hear.

Lucky Tray Day

In elementary school, once every month, you might
find a little slip of hot-pink paper on your lunch tray
and you would feel like you'd won the lottery—
you might get a kazoo or a neon pencil that said
light up the page!
or you might get a set of fuzzy stick-on mustaches.
It was luck of the draw, really,
but that day,
everyone in the cafeteria was your best friend because
of your
good luck.
No such luck now.
I look around the cafeteria and
wonder what everyone else did for New Year's,
wonder if anyone else has ever spent any time cleaning
up someone's throw-up,

wonder if they've ever watched their mom reach under
a teenage bed, feeling for almost-empty bottles of
alcohol—
a word that used to mean something else to me,
used to smell like the little square wipes they use right
before they shoot you in the arm with a needle
at the doctor's office.
Alcohol used to smell like the doctor's office in
general,
or maybe even like my grandpa's gin on the rocks,
a drink I sometimes bring him on a tray to be fancy,
the rocks wobbling against the glass as I go.
My tray wobbles now.
The new year is off to a shaky start.
James will go to a doctor now—not one with
antiseptic wipes, or shots,
but one who will give him
a shot at getting better,
at getting either back to how he used to be
or better at how he is now.
I look over at the long table, and Quinn looks at
me for a quick second and turns away, pretending
not to see, which I guess is what we all do from time
to time,

lucky to catch someone's attention some days,
lucky not to other days.
The old Quinn would stick on those mustaches with
me and pretend to be a detective or an old man and
we would crack up Lilly with our antics,
lucky to have gotten the hot-pink slip,
lucky to have gotten each other
in general.

Math Review

An estimate is an approximate number, Mr. Kaye
tells us,
a rough idea,
a guess.
I have three grandparents
and one step-grandparent,
so, roughly, four.
One beautiful and funny grandma who lives in
Florida and who makes me laugh and sends me new
boots every winter with a note that says
if you would move to Florida, you wouldn't need these,
you would only need flip-flops,
just sayin'
and every year I rip open the note and roll my eyes
and then I

roll out the big trunk where I keep all the old boots
she has gotten me, because I save the boots.
Mom says I could just save the notes,
but no.
I want the notes and I want the trunk of
boots too.
I also have two grandfathers and a tough-cookie
nana, all
on Dad's side,
all living right nearby and all taking turns visiting us
and coming to school concerts and
to our rescue.
My grandfathers are married to each other,
which is why I am surprised
that Dad is surprised
to find Mom with Jasmine,
which she told him officially in a short phone call just
last night,
in which he wasn't so nice.
I am starting to wonder if Dad would have been
surprised to find Mom with anyone at all—because it
can't be just because
Jasmine is a woman and Mom is a woman,

because we were all there when my grandfathers
walked down the aisle, just last year—
there when the rabbi wrapped the tallis around their
shoulders and when Mom squeezed Dad's hand,
because they sat next to each other,
Mom on one side of Dad and Stephanie on the other
side, because my family was starting to look like one
of those TV families,
right then.
And now—while we peek through the curtain to
estimate the attendance at the winter concert,
like they do at baseball games at big stadiums,
putting three guesses up on the big screen
during a pitching change—
Jackson asks
did your mom get it from your grandpa?
First guess is wrong!
Get what? I ask, thinking I never even met my mom's
dad and have only seen pictures, but thinking I for
sure got my green eyes from him, though.
You know. Isn't he married to a man? he asks.
Wrong grandfather, I say, laughing at his
miscalculation,

annoyed that Jackson thinks being gay is something
you can get,
like a virus,
proud of all the things I get from all the grandparents.
She didn't GET it from anyone, I say.
Who did YOUR mom get it from? I ask, even though
I hate the taste of those words coming out of my
mouth.
YOUR mom, he says,
and my mouth dries up and I cannot speak after that,
cannot even focus my eyes on the audience,
cannot sing one word of one wintry song,
and I LOVE these songs.
I strike out.
Jackson,
in my estimation,
is looking for someone to blame,
for this whole new
ball game.

Hardware

I hardly ever skip out on tech class, because we are
programming robots and I don't want to miss one bit
of that,
but sometimes I actually have to go,
not want to go.
This stall is clean except for one scribble,
a nursery rhyme.
Humpty Dumpty sat on a wall,
Humpty Dumpty had a great fall,
All the king's horses and all the king's men
Couldn't put Humpty together again.
Then there's a little doodle of a Humpty Dumpty
falling off the toilet, and under that,
Don't be Humpty Dumpty.
I chuckle.

Poor Humpty Dumpty, I think, wanting better things
for him.
Wanting him to be my robot so I can fix him all up.
I trace over him the way I traced over that first poem,
wanting things to be better for poor Nancy too.
I lift his weebly-wobbly
broken-egg body up and, squinting with one eye,
I can almost imagine him whole.

Animal Kingdom

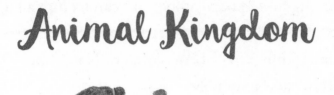

There is always a zoo trip in third grade, and you can't
wait because the zoo doesn't feel like school at all
because there are no desks and no spelling quizzes and
instead there is a wildlife scavenger hunt and
real live polar bears and
tropical birds and when you are eight years old,
wild animals are about as exciting as life gets.
So you go there on a crowded bus, with parent
chaperones and brown-bag lunches,
and you visit the monkeys and think for a quick
minute about Curious George
and the Man with the Yellow Hat,
and the balloons that carry George up and away
from the kids and the man, because you are eight and
Curious George is still kind of fresh in your mind.

And then you have lunch with your friends while the
parent chaperones drink iced coffees and
look at their watches,
and you and your group
run, run, run all over the place and stop in your tracks
because some animal handlers are throwing food at
some bears,
because it is feeding time,
and your heart is racing,
from racing around all day,
with your friends and their parents and their
schedules.
You don't stop to think for a minute about what the
animals *feel* like really, about what it *feels* like when
someone throws food at you through the bars in your
cage.
But then years later, you do.
Because years later,
the boy who called you Medusa in fourth grade,
the boy who touches your shoulder blades now,
had maybe touched your heart too,
who made you less afraid to look in a boy's eyes,
in anyone's eyes, really—

that boy brings you something at recess,
and it isn't a secret-admirer note like the one he and
his ANNOYING FRIENDS fake-sent you in
fourth grade,
an acrostic that spelled out your whole name,
ISABEL,
which you crumpled up in your backpack that day
but have kept in your porcelain keepsake box ever
since.
It isn't that but something else meaningful.
Dog food.
Because you are not Medusa anymore,
not Izzy either,
and especially not ISABEL.
You are a dog,
an animal
in a cage,
and you are suddenly
OBSESSED with those balloons and where you might
get some,
and what it might feel like to be lifted up high in the
sky above all of this,
curious if there is enough steam inside you to

take you
up and away
from this cage,
this rage,
this zoo.

Library

There shouldn't have been an outdoor recess in
February anyway,
which makes me wonder what Jackson would have
done with the dog food if we hadn't gone outside,
if we had been in the auditorium instead.
Would he have spread it out on the floor inside?
Sprinkled some in the hallway between classes?
I find myself in a bathroom stall for a change and
there is no writing here,
not one word,
just the closed-in quiet of tile floors and locked
doors,
and the trickle of a leaky faucet.
I wish there were a message to distract me or direct
me, but no.

I unlatch the door, wash my hands, and fling open the
door into the hallway, where there is a sign after all.
Lose Yourself in a Book,
and an arrow pointing to the library entrance.
I go inside and it smells and sounds like all libraries
everywhere—old carpet, crinkly plastic book jackets,
and whispers—
if it could be bottled up, I would buy it, spray it all
around my bedroom, and never come out
except for dinner.
Stargirl is on display at the main desk, and I pick it
up and wonder if rereading it for the millionth time
would do the trick.
Oh, you'll love that one, the librarian says.
I already do love it, I say.
So many kids find themselves in that book, she says,
smiling.
Find yourself in a book or lose yourself in a book,
which is it? I say.
I can tell from her smart eyes she knows what I mean,
knows that I am confused.
Depends what you're looking for, she says, and turns
back to her computer.

It's so quiet I almost jump out of my skin when I hear
the door fly open
and the bell rings
and there are loud hallway noises and shouting voices
and suddenly this whole crazy recess is over and I hear
someone say
¡vamanos! in a deep, rich voice and I turn around
to see a boy I've never seen before. He's tall and has
twinkly eyes and scars on his face and he's wearing a
sweater and a collared shirt and he's just
very different.
Is he talking to me?
Let's go, he says again, and my heart pounds because,
sure, I'll go anywhere right now because this feels
magical, surreal,
like *Stargirl.*
Coming! I hear behind me. *Chill!*
Another boy I've never seen brushes by and I'm
embarrassed all over again,
no dog food necessary.
He's very charming, the librarian says after they
disappear.
I stare at the door.

Are you okay? she asks,
and I realize I am not okay.
Both, I say.
I'm looking for both.
To be lost and to be found.

Pretend Play

Weekends sometimes come at the exact right time,
like magic,
right after someone brings you dog food at recess,
for example.
Ta-da!
Hey! a text pops onto my phone.
Lilly.
Hey!
And Quinn.
(Sometimes friends appear out of thin air like magic
too.)
A group chat with a group that
only exists here
on this phone,
like magic.

You are not a dog, texts Quinn.

You are NOT a dog, texts Lilly. *You are the prettiest*
person I know.

HEY, texts Quinn.

It's a tie, texts Lilly.

HAHA, I text.

This is all pretend anyway,

like when we were little, waving our

magic wands just for so,

just because it was three in the afternoon and there
were

wands that needed waving.

Pretend,

like when we

pretended we were in the no-friend club in fourth grade,

pretended that having no friends

together was better than having no friends

alone

and it worked.

That was the trick of the no-friend club in

Free to Be . . . You and Me too—

it waved its magic hippie wand over the whole fourth-

grade year and made it

magical.

Free to Be . . . You and Me and Jelly Bellys cast a spell
that year, and I want to text this to the group but I
keep it

to myself.

If I pretend and pretend

and pretend,

magic might happen again.

Let's get revenge, texts Lilly.

Nah, I text. *Not worth it,* I text again,

playing a trick on them and on

myself.

Maybe pretending to be cool

will make me cool,

the way a no-friend club made us,

like magic,

into the best of friends

in the first place,

or in the

fourth place.

I could go on like this, texting and texting and
texting—

the magic of talking without actually talking,

pretending to be cool and not

on fire

with nerves,

with shame,

with worry.

These phones are our new magic wands,

and we wave them around just for so,

just because it is three in the afternoon and there are

wands that need waving.

Fixer-Upper

We're going to buy a house, Isabel.
When my dad calls me Isabel, and not Izzy,
it is because he is nervous to tell me something.
It used to be that I was the only one who was nervous
around him,
and now he is always nervous around me,
afraid to tell me things, afraid to say
fixer-upper
about a house that he and Stephanie have already
bought,
not are *going to buy* like he said.
I think of Mom and the Formica countertops she
hates,
the ones that don't sparkle the way she hoped.
She always says this at Thanksgiving,

always looks down at them
as we clean up from a messy meal,
mad at them for being Formica in the first place and
not marble.
I worry about Dad and Stephanie fixing up a house.
I want to suggest Formica countertops,
so Stephanie can get mad at them too.
I am surrounded by fixer-uppers,
I think.
Mom, James,
Dad,
me.
Messy life,
cracked-up chin,
broken heart,
Humpty Dumptys
all of us.

Cha-Cha-Cha

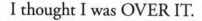

I thought I was OVER IT.

I thought that if I could get through the weekend and get to the other side of the INCIDENT, everyone would forget and NO ONE would ever speak of it again, but I WAS WRONG.

Did you know that the cha-cha-cha is called the cha-cha-cha because *cha-cha-cha*

sounds like the shuffling sound of our feet as we dance?

It is onomatopoeia,

a noise for a word,

like the *BOOM!*

and *POW!*

of my fist hitting Jackson's face

for saying on the bus

that the dog food was a joke,
for saying that I don't know how to TAKE a joke,
that maybe I am gay too, because it seems to
RUN IN MY FAMILY,
for saying that Quinn definitely is not gay because she
kissed him on the cheek during spin the bottle.
Jackson is apparently
dumber than I thought, since he seems to forget
that both my mom and HIS MOM were married to
actual men
in the first place,
forget a kiss on the stupid cheek
during stupid spin
the stupid bottle.
So because he is a pig,
OINK
(but worse because he is not cute and pink like an
actual pig),
I growled OUT LOUD
this morning,
GRRRRR,
when I woke up to
the fact that I would be face to face

with his face.

Aargh.

One-two-three,

cha-cha-cha,

became

I-hate-him,

cha-cha-cha,

and there I was,

forced to dance with him, forced to see that people do
not change,

that what I thought was friendship, or something else,

was something else still,

and before I know it,

I am transported to a faraway place where there is no
Jackson,

no dog food,

no group chats,

no FaceTime,

just actual faces and actual time and

waves

CRASHING onto the beach

while I *Ommmmm*

my way out of the

dancing
classroom,
down the stairs,
and out the—
SLAM—
door.
No more turnoffs or rest stops.
No slowing down.
No safe driving and eggs over medium-low heat.
I am done.
I see blue hair and tequila in my future.
One-two-three,
cha-cha-cha.

Dear Diary

Mom says sometimes you feel all the feelings at once,
and now I know what that means.
One minute you don't feel anything at all, and the next
minute—smack in the middle of the cha-cha-cha—
you feel
ALL OF THEM,
flitting around your insides,
taking you to a wide-awake place where the sun is in
your eyes,
where you are
sadder than you realized,
madder too,
realizing that you have
HAD IT
too.

And that one big push,
the satisfying *ker-clunk* the school door made when it
locked back into place,
locking inside of it Jackson Allen, and Quinn Mitchell
and Heidi, and Fiona and Sara, and all the new kids
you don't even know yet
but who will maybe hurt you
soon enough anyway, since it seems like this place
brings out the worst in people—
seems like they all left the better versions of
themselves back in that time capsule we created at
Salem Ridge.
I flew—like a butterfly,
outside of myself and
down that school driveway,
where I found myself face to face with the daily life of
grown-ups—
their busy streets, their cars going by,
the women and their
baby strollers and their chitchat and sighs,
the people across the street at that store,
loading groceries into their loaded-up cars and looking
harried and tired, and suddenly

I felt harried and tired too.

I felt bad about how much trouble this would cause
and it did,

dear diary.

Except that I made it all the way home and so did
Mom and so did Dad because the school scared them
both so much they had to be in the same room—
the kitchen—

to talk about me.

Not James and his tequila problem, not Mom and her
girlfriend problem—is that a problem?

Not Dad's wedding and his swing dancing and angry-
handwriting problem,

but me.

But James took me for a walk—

back to Salem Ridge to cool off,

because Dad was shouting at Mom and she was
shouting back and

James saying

let's go and grabbing me by the hand made me feel
protected a little,

from the sounds of years and fights past,

made me feel like he might pat my head, even.

Are you going to throw jelly beans at the wall? James
asks, and I know what he means and I WANT to.
This is a jelly-beans-against-the-wall moment if ever
there was one.
If I HAD jelly beans, and especially if I had
WATERMELON Jelly Bellys,
the best ones, the ones I gave to Quinn at the
end-of-year picnic in fourth grade, which basically
made them
FRIENDSHIP Jelly Bellys,
well, I would throw them at this brick wall where all
the boys used to play wall ball after school and where
James would sometimes pick me up and walk me to
my singing lesson and now that's all gone so,
YES, I WOULD THROW JELLY BELLYS, JAMES,
if I could,
and would you scoop them back up for me, like you
did,
and save them for me for when I really need to know
that someone is cleaning up after me, the way I
clean up after everyone else?
We sit and throw rocks at the wall instead,
and Mom and Dad drive up and James walks off with

Dad, and Mom takes my hand and I tell her about
the dog food and she puts her arm around me and
tells me
well that's a doggone good story,
and ha ha, I suppose it is.
I tell her about Quinn too, and the makeup, and
not-mountain-Heidi, and she says *wow, you remember*
all that Heidi stuff? The wooden shoes and the book and
the movie?
Wow.
And then says *things are changing, huh?*
And I nod and she says
I used to be your diary, and I nod again,
and she says *I fell down on the job,* and I nod again,
and she says
I am back.
I am your diary.
Your stuff is safe with me.
Dear Diary, I say.
I want to go back to the way things used to be.
Dear Izzy, she says,
you can't go back. The only way through is forward, so
maybe just choose some

little pieces of the past to take with you for good luck.
Like a time capsule, I say,
happy I have a diary that writes back.
Yup, she says. *Exactly like that.*

Group Chat

Jackson: *My mom says I have to apologize.*
Izzy: *You don't have to.*
Jackson: *I want to.*
Pause.
Izzy: *Okay.*
Quinn: *I am here too.*
Pause.
Jackson: *I added her. You are not a dog.*
A number I don't know: *Hi.*
Quinn: *I added Heidi.*
Pause. I am mad at Quinn, I realize now,
for adding Heidi right now and
in the first place.
Mad at her for leaving me behind,
for letting her spin land on Jackson,

really mad except it's not her fault for moving on.

It feels more like my fault for staying put.

Izzy: *Hi.*

Lilly: *Hi.*

Izzy: *I added Lilly.*

Loyal Lilly.

Jackson: *Well, so can I tell my mom it's fine?*

Izzy: *It's fine.*

It is NOT fine.

Lilly: *You're the dog, Jackson, but yeah, okay, it's fine.*

Loyal Lilly.

Quinn: *Nice, Lilly.*

Heidi: *Okay, bye!*

Izzy: *Bye.*

Lilly: *See ya.*

Quinn: *Later.*

Pause.

Jackson: *Izzy?*

Izzy: *Why'd you add me back in?*

Jackson: *I was embarrassed about our moms.*

Izzy: *Maybe I am too.*

Jackson: *Are we related now?*

Izzy: *Don't make me laugh. I'm still REALLY mad.*

Jackson: *Sis?*

Izzy: *STOP.*

Jackson: *Sorry.*

Izzy: *Did you just wake up in the morning and decide to bring dog food?*

Jackson: *I don't know. Yes. I was mad.*

Izzy: *And that helped?*

Jackson: *No.*

Izzy: *Do you like Quinn?*

Jackson: *Kind of. Sorry.*

Izzy: *It's okay. I like her too.*

I do. I always have and I always will.

Izzy: *(Not THAT way!)*

Jackson: *Ha ha.*

Izzy: *Later.*

Jackson: *Bye.*

Detention

Lilly and Quinn and I walk down the hall from last
period and I peek inside the room where I will be
detained for the next hour—
Lilly and Quinn and I is a phrase I haven't used all
year long until this minute,
and I imagine our moms chitchatting carefully about
what has become of
the three of us.
Then I imagine my mom telling their moms about her
and Jackson's mom, because she wanted to tell them
so they didn't hear it through the grapevine,
a grown-up version of whisper down the alley—
and I imagine Quinn's mom, in particular, feeling
shocked but pretending not to be and telling Quinn
she should

make more of an effort with me,
make my walk to after-school detention more of a
group effort maybe.
I don't mind the interference,
don't mind having them by my side,
don't mind it at all because I know it won't last.
Mom would say this is what nostalgia feels like, I bet.
It's a missing feeling, really.
I'll have to catch up on what I missed, as if it were a
sick day,
and all because I got a little carried away with my
cha-cha-cha
and skipped right out of the school day with no
permission slip in sight,
a funny thing to do, when I'm the one who's usually
sticking around for too long.
And now I am not allowed to do much but think
about what I did,
not allowed to read, just think.
Lucky I have other things to catch up on,
like how to turn a tango into a paper about my ideal
civilization,
to somehow combine

our ballroom dance with regular social studies,
and so far I've only learned how long it takes to
get from school to home in the middle of a historic
temper tantrum.
The clock ticks and I actually wish it would go slower.
Sometimes being made to sit still in one place—
sometimes not having to call anyone or make any
plans or wonder
who is doing what with whom—
isn't a punishment at all.
It's a reward.

Foreign Exchange

We have a guest speaker in Spanish class today,
a boy from Spain
whose name is Mateo,
whose accent is special
because it is from Spain,
and not Latin America, like Señora Navalón's
pretty accent.
It reminds me of my old lisp,
something I got rid of in kindergarten the minute
I had
gotten rid of New York City
in exchange for this town,
the minute I realized my lisp might be a problem
one day.
Got rid of it all on my own,
determined not to have any problems besides

not wanting my mom to leave me

in that school with all those kids I had never seen
before,

some of them with lisps, none of them

willing to

risk

making me their friend, except one.

Lilly (with two *l*'s)

and no lisp.

But this Spanish boy and his

ACCENT.

Mom would say he was charming,

his blue eyes lighting up the room,

the ugly scars on his face making his other features
seem especially

not ugly.

He is the boy from the library.

My name is Mateo, he says, giving us a nickname right
away.

I come from eh-Spain, he says,

giving us a laugh with his funny little accent, telling us
all about paella—the signature dish of his country—
which is basically a mess of different foods all thrown
in a pot,

and it sounds spicy and overwhelming and
like something I would never ever want to eat.
Mateo is a seventh grader,
visiting our country for a year,
an exchange program,
though I don't know what he gets
in exchange for being here,
kids chuckling at his broken English,
bullying boys buckling their knees behind his to make
him feel
unstable
here?
But no.
He is a soccer star, flipping the ball off his head and
into the goal
like it is nothing,
I hear the boys whisper behind me.
Do it again, I hear them say after school, out by the
soccer field,
while we walk toward town.
No one gets bullied when they have the exact thing
everyone else wants.
Blue eyes,

dark hair that flips when he turns back to me
and,
like a star,
smiles his crooked teeth
at me.
My heart tells me he is here to
exchange
an old lisp for a new one,
maybe an old crush
for a new one
too.

Run-On Sentence

Mr. Marks says life is a run-on sentence, and if you
don't learn
how to punctuate it,
how to pace it, you'll be
too out of breath
to tell a good story.
We're supposed to write about a moment when
something changed, a teeny, tiny little moment when
something big came from something small.
And all I can think of is tacos.
There was once a taco night when Dad came for Mom
in a new convertible sports car, in which he took her
for a ride,
even though it was cold,
because he was excited,
and I thought everything was going to go back to normal,

and Dad would come home, and we would have taco
night
after taco night
together as an
average family with a sports car and Mexican
condiments,
but Mom came home mad,
slamming the car door and the front door and,
later,
the bedroom door,
and I realize now that we haven't had a taco night
since, that
the end of taco night was
the beginning of everything else—
the beginning of Dad and Stephanie,
the beginning of Mom and Jasmine,
of James and his blue hair,
his tequila, the Mexican condiment I hadn't
thought of,
the beginning of Quinn and Heidi,
Mateo and his accent and his eyes,
Jackson and Quinn,
and how
everything else

that happened after taco night has been
messy and overwhelming,
and I think that in two short years,
Mom has a girlfriend,
Dad has a fiancée,
James has a drinking-tequila problem,
and I have a crush on a boy from Spain,
the same boy the whole school
has a crush on,
even the boys,
which means he will never see me,
which means
Mom will have Jasmine,
Dad will have Stephanie,
Jackson will have Quinn,
Heidi will have the long table,
James will have tequila,
and I will have nothing,
which means that
everything else
basically
has turned to paella.
Out of breath is right.

Crossing Guard

We have to crisscross this building so many times
during the day that I get tired thinking about it in the
morning,
racing around, so little time to get from one thing to
the next,
people coming at you from all angles,
things flying at you too, when someone throws
someone a water bottle across the crowded hall,
for example.
I have learned to cross through the cafeteria to get to
art class,
a shortcut
that saves me two whole minutes of the four I've got,
and I wouldn't normally waste them,
unless there was someone hunched over and crying

behind the vending machine and you go to check on
her, and she,
the hunched-over girl,
is Heidi,
and I've got two minutes to figure out if this is
something worth being late for.
It all happens so fast after that, and with a little tap on
the shoulder she is a fountain,
sobbing.
She is failing everything, she says,
she doesn't get anything, she says,
wants to just go home because she is so dumb,
and I've got one more minute to tell her I will help her
anytime,
that I am not good at lip gloss but very good at math,
and *excelente* at Spanish,
and that I am in between extracurricular activities
(and friends) and can definitely help,
and I tell her that anyone who is friends with the great
Quinn Mitchell
is anything but dumb,
that Quinn Mitchell is the marshmallow-and-pretzel-
stick-building champion of Salem Ridge Elementary,

and I get her to stand up and smile and she agrees to
take help and also a sip of water and I get to class in
the nick of time and think that
really so many objects can cross your path around here
they should maybe think about a crossing guard—
looking out for flying water bottles and
other things you don't see coming.

# Lightbulb

All this time, Lilly's been sitting in the second lunch
with a girl named Ginger, whose name sounds like it
belongs in one of Mr. De Marzo's cooking lessons
and whose face is brown and full
and who wears her hair in one million teeny braids
that fall down her back and make a satisfying and
noiseless
noise,
and all I want to do is reach out and touch them,
and who, whenever I run into her with my old friend
Lilly,
smiles at me, and today I run smack into them right
after I run smack into Mateo—SMACK into him—
our actual bodies walking one way while our heads
are turned another,

and he says *sorry,* but he rolls his *r*'s, and I want to
say *it's okay* but then I hear Ginger laughing and Lilly
shushing her,
and I can't believe I have run SMACK into Mateo just
a few days after I even know who Mateo is in the first
place,
but suddenly he is everywhere.
Mateo, Mateo, Mateo.
It's okay, says Lilly, giving me a push like the push
toward the long table I gave Quinn way back,
and I am a little closer to him than I mean to be and
he says *see you, Ee-sa-bel* and walks away and
I swear . . .
I am speechless.
And then I am not.
He is so much cuter than Jackson, I say.
And he speaks Spanish AND English, I say, and *he is a
star soccer player,* I say.
And he even smiles in Spanish.
Wait, Jackson? Lilly asks.
Did you like-like Jackson?
And I say *no*
and she says *good, because he definitely likes Quinn and*

because whoa, your moms, and also, I think of you two
as good friends,
which hits me
SMACK
in the middle of the stomach that friends is what we
are,
or were.
It is like someone turned on the light right there in
the hallway.
BUT MATEO! I whisper, and I realize I haven't told
Lilly much, that I have been thinking more than I
have been talking and that when you talk,
everyone talks back,
and suddenly,
you have friends.
Ginger starts to laugh so hard she screams,
like I do,
and then she says *oh my God, I'm sorry I overlaughed,*
and I think *overlaughing* is the perfect word for what
she does,
and that here at this moment,
smack in the middle of a regular middle school day,
a lightbulb turned on and I turned back on too.

Invitation

It's funny how a piece of mail can sock you in the
stomach as if it were someone's fist, or a bag of dog
food sprinkled out on the ground for all to see.
I wanted to hide it from Mom, the same way I
wanted to hide from Lilly and Ginger that I had
been invited to hang out at Heidi's on Friday after
school
and they had not.
I know Heidi only invited me because I helped her
with Spanish,
because I gave her my tricks for remembering the
capitals,
tricking her into believing that there is a boy named
Santiago who is chilly
in Chile,

because when we make something into an interesting story,

not fact but fiction,

that something becomes permanent

in our minds.

Like poor Santiago who is chilly.

Heidi won't forget him, I know it.

So I got an invite but Lilly and Ginger did not,

and Jasmine did not get an invite either.

I am the first to know this, because I always meet the mail carrier in person in case something important is coming—a thick white envelope with calligraphy on the outside, silver lining, and Hebrew letters in foil and a date that will become an anniversary on the inside. Important indeed.

I tried to hide it but Mom saw it peeking out from under the fruit bowl and just tapped the corner of the hefty envelope and stood there

and I felt I could hear her heart beating out of her chest,

or maybe it was mine.

She never even looked inside. Just picked up her phone and left a message,

the kids will be there, but I will not,
sending a message that she was not alone anymore,
that she was a we, that it was either both of them or
neither of them.
Which was an invitation to me, I know,
to be more inviting too.

Appointment

I sit and watch the boys play soccer while I wait for
James and Mom to come get me for the orthodontist,
and I look away when Mateo looks in my direction,
because I am afraid I will mix things up and
don't want to mistake
friendly for flirting and
find myself in a pile of dog food all over again.
James's main punishment for drinking
is having to spend more time with us,
which I think isn't really punishment, because we are
charming and we make him laugh and his real hair
color seems to be growing in, which means maybe he's
getting real again.
Jackson comes toward me and I realize he's probably
coming with us too—
all of us in one car all the time lately,

all of us at the orthodontist to get my braces off.
One big happy family.
And I think that Jackson still looks like fourth-grade
Jackson sometimes, especially when a seventh grader
named Mateo grabs his arm and they both come
toward me and I
brace myself.
Hello, Ee-sa-bel, Mateo says,
and Jackson steps back and juggles a soccer ball and I
hear Mom's laugh behind me, announcing herself the
way only Mom can.
Hi, she shouts at the top of her lungs, *I'm Ee-sa-bel's
mom,* she shouts.
Hi, Mateo says, flashing a smile that is not straight,
but perfect.
I am Mateo and I am eh-Spanish, he says,
I am not eh-deaf.
We all laugh so hard in that moment,
the butterflies are not in my belly at all, they are in my
throat,
and Mom says *James is in the car* and I say *okay* and
stare at the grass as they all walk away and I turn to
walk away too, but Mateo reaches out for my hand
a little

and I let him take it a little
and he asks *is it okay if I will text you?*
And I nod and say *¡sí!*
with the exclamation points in the right places and
the accent on the *i* in my head, because I want him to
know I pay attention in Spanish class,
that I know where the accents and the exclamation
points go,
that I know the capital of España
(with the tilde over the *n*)
is Madrid.
I'm getting my braces off today, I say, and flash him a
metallic smile and walk away.
¡Hasta luego! I shout,
¡Hasta pronto! he shouts,
and I pull out my phone the second I get in the car,
so I can learn
right away
that *pronto* means *soon,*
and I
brace myself
for soon.

Formica

I stand in the old-fashioned kitchen with Dad and
Stephanie and pretend to admire the house they are
fixing up,
smiling when I'm supposed to,
mmm-hmm-ing about the things they will do to
make it perfect.
Just perfect, says Stephanie, who is always cheerful and
positive
and hates Formica countertops
as much as Mom does, as it turns out, and
simply will not have it.
James is upstairs scouting out a room for himself, and
I try to find room to say something important in a sea
of unimportant renovation information.
Why didn't you invite Jasmine? I ask, and now I am

certain it is my heart pounding because I live in fear
of Dad's angry handwriting turning into
angry other things.
I hear James come down the stairs and slowly inch his
way back up and
away from this.
Seems unnecessary, no? Dad says, and he goes back to
opening and closing the cabinets he will soon replace
with newer ones.
*It didn't seem unnecessary to have Mom at Grandpa's
wedding,* I say. *She even held your hand there, even after
you left us.*
Isabel. He says my name in the final way he says
things sometimes. *It should be obvious to you now that
maybe I had no chance.*
This is Dad's angry side and
I wonder if Stephanie wants to renovate that too.
I think back to what my house used to feel like—
Dad's temper filling up the whole place,
making the air feel either light or heavy,
depending only on him,
so maybe Mom found Jasmine and her yoga and her
deep breathing steady and soft and open and kind,

and maybe Mom just really needed a person who
always
asked how her day was,
maybe the fact that she was a woman
wasn't the point at all.
Maybe Mom loves Jasmine as a person,
and it doesn't matter if she's a man or a woman.
I don't think that's true, I say to Dad now. I want to
say more things about this but I'm afraid I will throw
up if I do, so I keep my dry mouth shut and wait.
I'm happy to invite them both, Stephanie says now, her
hand on my shoulder.
Thank you, I say.
You and Mom have a lot in common, you know?
Oh, like what?
You both hate Formica.

Plans

But we made a plan, I say into the phone to Lilly and
Ginger,
because we are on a speakerphone conference call,
planning to go to the big group hangout after school
on Friday.
We decided we don't want to go, says Lilly, and I realize
that lately,
some other two people are always the *we,*
and never someone else and me.
I also know that I could be part of the *we* if I didn't
want to go somewhere they didn't want to go,
but I do,
do want to see what all the fuss is about,
what it feels like to be invited in.
You go, Ginger says, *and come back and tell us all about
it, and ESPECIALLY if they play spin the bottle!*

Ginger loves drama,
loves a lot of things, including Lilly and me.
Meeting someone like her makes me wonder how I
ever lived life without someone like her.
No wonder I felt lonely and confused.
I did not have a Ginger, who makes the same old
things feel exciting and funny,
makes it okay to be weird,
okay to have crushes, makes the things that are
unfamiliar and uncomfortable
when I am alone with them
feel familiar and comfortable
when I am with her.
She even started calling me Spot because I told her
about the dog food and Lilly tried to stop her but I
love having a nickname,
and love that Lilly tried to stop her
and love that, okay,
maybe the three of us are a we.
Sounds like a plan, Lilly says, excited for me to go, and
this makes me feel okay enough about going with Quinn,
who seems a little more interested in me now that
Heidi is interested in me, which is okay with me, since
I'll always be interested in Quinn.

We are bonded by Jelly Bellys and *Stargirl*. Those are forever bonds.

Shoot, I say when I hang up and find Mom looking at me.

Things don't always work out the way you planned, Iz.

Clearly, I say.

Did you plan this? I ask Mom, waving my hand around in wild circles as if that will help her know that I mean her and Jasmine.

But she does know what I mean, because she always knows what I mean.

She laughs.

I didn't plan it at all, she says,

but I didn't NOT plan it either.

Do you think that's why Dad has mad handwriting? I say, and Mom laughs.

I think he always had mad handwriting, to be honest, she says,

and I feel bad if I've made it madder.

But you're going? I ask.

We are, she says, and

there's that *we* again.

Seems like Stephanie is a better influence on him than I was, she says.

Stephanie has big plans for that house, I say.

We all have big plans for something, she says. *It's what you do when the big plans don't work out that helps you figure out who you are.*

I am afraid to ask but I can't help it.

Isn't this who you always were?

Her chest puffs up with breath and she exhales a big *yes.*

It is. This is who I always was, I just like her more now.

I like her too, I say.

And by the way, she says. *Spin the bottle?*

Don't worry, I say.

My big plan is to run home if that happens!

I've figured out that much.

Scavenger Hunt

We go looking for Heidi's house,
Quinn and me,
because Heidi is having a get-together on a Friday
afternoon and
all of a sudden Heidi and Quinn are telling me
things, my eyes darting around my own phone the
way Quinn's do when we FaceTime,
looking for something else.
As we turn corners, the streets get wider, and we find
ourselves in a place we haven't been before,
looking for something we don't know yet
if we really want,
and I half expect Heidi's house to be a cabin in the
Swiss Alps,
a grumpy old grandpa waiting for her to return to him,

a girl in a wheelchair waiting for her to tap-dance for
her,
like Shirley Temple does in *Heidi,* the movie,
but Grandfather is not there, and no rich girl in a
wheelchair either.
Heidi seems to be the rich girl here.
Her house,
I find,
is a mansion on a flat street not far from school,
where she was just crying the other day because she
felt bad about herself,
but her HOUSE is a MANSION.
And her babysitter is a teenager who I have seen
before,
someone James knows, I think.
Her picture shows up on his phone sometimes and his
smile
shows up about the same time.
The tips of her blue hair match the blue of James's hair
and I wonder if
I have found his girlfriend,
wonder also if she loves tequila so much it is worth
throwing up for,

wonder if Heidi's mom knows that Heidi's babysitter
is friends with a guy like James, or if
she finds blue
a cool color for hair,
the way I find Heidi
a cool name for a sixth grader,
the way this mansion is
a cool way to have a house.
We find boys and snacks waiting for us,
Jackson looking the other way when we walk in,
finding himself torn probably
between his mom's girlfriend's daughter
and his girlfriend.
Go, I say, as I do now all the time with Quinn,
and I find my way upstairs to Heidi's room,
where it is lavender and gigantic, and where there are
bright white shutters
and a four-poster bed, and where
I find,
there on her desk, an old-fashioned-looking copy of
Heidi, the book,
and a pair of wooden shoes sitting on top.
And I find myself laughing—overlaughing—

alone in a lavender room.
All year long I have been
thinking about this other Heidi,
the one from the book,
the curly-haired, singing-and-dancing girl from the
movie,
the Heidi who makes everyone feel better about
everything,
and secretly I have found her.
She has been here the whole time.

Solid, Liquid, Gas

I take off my shoes
because I'm doing Jasmine a solid,
sitting down with her and Jackson on this mat in the
sunroom,
grounding myself in my pose, feeling the solid earth
beneath me
while James plays football in the backyard with Jesse
and the two of them tumble to the ground also, the
solid earth beneath them.
And now for the first time I realize
even James's name matches theirs.
I take in a deep breath because Jasmine tells us to in a
voice that is meant to soothe, but which feels scratchy
and nervous,
like it is gearing up to say something less obvious than

BREATHE.

I let the air out purposefully because Jasmine believes
that the air we let out should be as meaningful as the
air we let in,
and I can't help thinking Jackson and I are
breathing each other's air,
when we used to breathe as far away as possible from
each other.
This is what it feels like to let go of everything that
goes on outside of this space, to block it out and make
this a safe space.
Can you feel that, Izzy?
Can you feel that, Jackson?
This is going to work for us, I can feel it.
Jasmine assumes we are an *us* the same way Stephanie
says she is an *extra mom.*
I think I have two moms too many.
We straighten out our backs and lengthen our necks
and I peek open one eye at her and wonder how
someone as calm and collected,
as solid as she is, could have given an unruly Jackson
Allen to this world.
She peeks open one eye too and catches me

and her mouth turns up on one side, smiling,
as I realize that my feelings about her are fluid,
like my friendship with Quinn, and even my
friendship with Jackson—flowing in and out of the
spaces in each other's lives when there is
a space to fill.
One more downward dog, she says,
and we do as she says and I look under my armpit at
Jackson, who is looking at me, so I bark at him and he
laughs and we fall out of our poses,
landing on solid ground.

Chaperones

You GUYS! I laugh.
Lilly and Ginger unpack a picnic basket—
egg salad sandwiches cut with cookie cutters
into the shape of stars,
cucumber sticks,
and Hershey's chocolate bars—
Lilly FaceTimed Ginger three times last night to
remind her to
put the chocolate in the freezer so it wouldn't melt
on our date.
All my friends had to hear was Mateo saying to me,
under the stairwell, at dismissal yesterday,
that he would be at this park today for a soccer game,
that he hoped I would be there too, and—
It's a date!

It's not a date.
It's a date!
It's not a date.
We went back and forth about it until we decided
a heat wave was a perfect time to go on a pretend
picnic
to watch a soccer game of a boy who would probably
be leaving to go back to eh-Spain
forever—
para siempre—
any minute now.
I want to go back to the air-conditioning of Ginger's
dad's car, but Ginger's dad had some errands to run so
we're stuck here,
sticking to a wool blanket I pulled out of Dad's musty
hall closet.
It is itchy and uncomfortable, and of course it is—
Dad's not such a comfortable guy.
All set, Ginger says, crossing her arms and admiring
her setup.
The only thing missing is a bottle, Lilly says, obsessed
with spin the bottle
as an extracurricular activity.

No bottle, no spinning! Sorry, Charlie, I say, shrugging
in a giant, dramatic shrug
and feeling comfortable in my own skin again,
even on that
itchy, comfort-
less
blanket.
Okay, okay, we need a picture!
We spin around and Ginger hoists her arm way above
us and is about to take the picture when I see him in
the camera,
walking toward us in his cleats, smiling,
his friends carrying flowers,
Mateo carrying
two bottles of orange soda.
Bottles!
Lilly squeezes my hand.
It's totally a date.

Walkers

We line up, my brother and me,
on either side of my dad,
who seems nervous and happy,
and we walk,
not over crunchy leaves,
like the day he said he was
leaving,
but over a white cloud of an aisle,
the grass holding it up,
with its springtime crunch.
We get to the front,
we hug Stephanie and move to the side, where James,
who is pierced through and through,
angry, sometimes drunk,
sometimes throwing up,

sometimes flying over the handlebars,
sometimes listening to the Beatles and looking up at
the stars,
takes my hand.
Try not to cry, he says, his hand scolding me with its
squeeze.
I look out at my mom and Jasmine,
and Jackson, the dog-food-spreading
dog of a person,
old enemy,
new friend,
is here, holding his mother's hand
who is holding my mother's hand.
That walking felt slow,
the ceremony feels quick.
Just like that it's over,
done.
I didn't cry.
There will be a big party now, under a tent,
with punch and an omelet station, and
James and I walk behind Dad and Stephanie and the
grass crunches more,
and we say *oh, hi!* and *thank you!*

as we meet and greet all the people we know already and

all the ones we don't—Stephanie's people, mostly.

And there's beachy music playing, and a DJ holding out a microphone

in my direction and

my dad asks me to go on and sing something for everyone and

I'm not prepared for any of this.

Go on, Iz, James says,

and he throws his arm over my shoulders,

pulling my hair too tight,

and he walks me up to the microphone,

some tears springing into my eyes

flinching

at the pinch of my hair,

but I'm afraid if I let go,

he will inch away

from me again,

when I have just gotten him back.

But I do let go,

and I take the microphone, look out at my family,

and sing.

We're Going on a Bear Hunt

Dad calls me from the airport,
something he's never done once in his life.
He and Stephanie are off on their honeymoon,
off to an exotic locale,
not San Juan, Puerto Rico,
not San Jose, Costa Rica either.
A medical conference in
San Diego, California.
I am off to camp in a week,
was on the hunt for some LIGHT READING for
nighttime,
when the phone rang.
I keep thinking of your song, he says.
Keep thinking that I almost got a case of cold feet, he says.

Almost didn't get to hear you sing to us.
I raise my eyebrows, imagining Stephanie standing there,
left high and dry under the chuppah.
I feel terrible just thinking about what his
cold feet might have done to her.
Feel terrible that sometimes when Dad picks us up for
a night at his house,
looking tired and handsome in his surgical greens,
when I am off gathering my backpack and overnight
bag,
he and Mom laugh at something inside,
something just between them,
and I let myself imagine them sitting
like regular parents
on the sofa,
arguing over what to watch,
and I feel this strange relief.
How'd you get over it? I ask.
It's like the bear hunt book, he says.
There's no way around it.
You have to go through it.
I laugh.
The bear hunt book.

He read it to me so many times.
We pretended we were them, an adventuresome
family with fire in our eyes and
courage in our bones.
A river! We can't go over it.
We can't go under it.
We have to go THROUGH it.
Splash splosh!
The only cure for cold feet is to move your feet forward,
he says.
Warms 'em right up.
Like the cha-cha-cha, I think.
Have a great honeymoon, I say and we hang up and I
see Mom and Jasmine
hanging up a picture of Jackson and me from
Halloween,
and I am relieved to be
relieved to be
moving forward,
over the moon,
actually.
We're going on a bear hunt.
We're not scared.

Civilization

The all-school social is a little more formal than the
sixth-grade mixer, and especially
if you are from eh-Spain, where middle school boys
wear pants with belts and buttoned-up shirts and
cologne that smells like a mixture of camp and
waterfalls—Niagara, even.
I go with Lilly and Ginger and we send Quinn a selfie
and she sends one back
and we dance near each other,
in separate circles,
but dressed up in equal parts lip gloss and
looking out for each other.
If I had to invent my own civilization, everyone would
speak a combination of Florida grandma and
Spanish from Spain and

we would all leave our mark in funny ways,
inside library books,
and in gum stuck under the table at Mario's Pizza,
in the instructional dance footprints of our favorite
social studies teacher,
locked inside the tight grip of girls' hands holding
hands,
old friends and new,
and also in other ways,
where you have to excuse yourself from the
knee-sliding,
body-slamming dance circle for a sec,
where you might tell everyone at the dance you'll be
right back,
that you have to go to the bathroom to put on some
more gloss,
not too much,
and you will squeeze around the long table,
pretending to yourself that's true,
and you might pretend to pull out of your cross-body
bag
the exact right kind of sparkly lip gloss the how-to
article recommended,

now that you finally got around to reading it,
the one your grandfathers slipped into your hand
because your mom wasn't so sure, because you had on
just enough already,
but you leave it there now and go into a stall and
grab on to something else—
a medium-point green Sharpie—
you take some mindful breaths and prepare yourself
for your civilization's
highest ritual,
and you might draw a little palm tree and sign your
name,
leave your mark—
Izzy was here—
and then you will go on your way,
your face hot,
your feet
a little less
cold,
the stall door bouncing behind you,
because civilization awaits,
and you've got some bouncing to do too.

author's note

When you are a Jewish girl growing up in a small Pennsylvania town in the early 1980s and you find out your dad is gay, life gets a little more complicated. And if you happen to be in middle school, *complicated* is a bit of an understatement. I would know. That girl was me. As a budding writer with a knack for collecting emotions and ambience, I tucked a lot of that childhood experience away for later use. At the start of my writing career, when I was figuring out what I wanted to say, I tried my best to unpack it by writing a version of *The Cure for Cold Feet* that was closer to my own story. But the novel was nostalgic and played out in a bubble of time. I hadn't gotten it quite right. I put it in a drawer the way writers do, intending to try again, to revisit and revise it one day.

As time marched on, children's publishing started to evolve into a more inclusive place, where more and more writers could tell their stories in their own voices. In this brave new space, that novel in my drawer started to feel more like historical fiction and less like the realistic, contemporary fiction it was meant to be. Suddenly, it became extremely important to me to tell my story as if it were happening *this* year, in 2018. Things would have to be different. Izzy would get to live in a more fluid, much more inclusive world than I did.

When I work with students on their small-moments writing, I encourage them to close their eyes and see and smell and feel the memory so that they can find the right words to capture it. I was able to use this very exercise when I wrote Izzy's recollection of her grandfathers' wedding, because her memory is my memory. Izzy gets to reflect on a beautiful image of two men in an embrace, a tallis wrapped around them under a chuppah, as if it were nothing terribly new or shocking. When my home state, Pennsylvania, finally made it legal for my dad to marry his longtime life partner, I got to bear witness to progress and love and understanding. Izzy, like my own daughter, who sat beside me that day, is a generation removed and is therefore allowed to feel unencumbered pride and love for her grandfathers. That's not to say Izzy isn't capable of nuanced feelings—she still feels all the normal and complicated feelings about her mother's new relationship, to be sure. But her reaction is stripped of most of the fear and worry I felt about my dad's homosexuality so long ago.

I'm incredibly grateful for the writers and editors who have given children and parents and educators the opportunity to see their stories represented in ways that feel authentic. All of this has freed me up to write this book in this particular way. I am so grateful for this opportunity, and grateful also for an insightful and supportive editor in Michelle Nagler, who believes wholeheartedly in Izzy's story and who pushed me to find ways to make her more and more real, more herself. I'm thankful for Jill Grinberg, my agent, who has always believed in my ability to tell stories like this one. And, as I always say, I am grateful for my mom, my dad, and my brother, who allow me to be creative with my memories, and whose love for each other has transcended some of life's more challenging moments and made us a strong and funny and weird family that I couldn't possibly write well enough in fiction.

As Izzy starts to branch out in middle school and starts to find her voice and her people and her place, I took as inspiration all the good friends who have made me feel understood and who have also expanded my worldview along the way, starting way back in high school when I met a certain Spanish-speaking exchange student whose accent and sense of humor opened me up to a whole world outside rural Pennsylvania and set me on a path of looking around myself with wide-open eyes.

Thanks are in order to all the incredible people who make books happen, but especially to Jenna Lettice and Leslie Mechanic at Random House and to Katelyn Detweiler at Jill Grinberg Literary. Thank you also to the educators who have found ways to incorporate mindfulness and "butterfly moments" into their small-moments writing work, and who work hard to bring verse writing into the lives of children. Thank you to the librarians who stock books with all kinds of stories inside so that kids may always, as Izzy discovers, find themselves or lose themselves in a book, as need be. Thanks also to my brilliant husband, Jon Ain, my first reader and my own personal cheering section, and to my children, Grace and Elijah, who, at their very young ages, see the world as an anything-can-happen place, and whose warm and open hearts help thaw out my cold feet every day.

beth ain

grew up in Allentown, Pennsylvania, where she got cold feet trying to figure out how to open her locker, waiting backstage at the talent show, and on thousands of other occasions throughout middle school. She was lucky to have had some special friends and a not-so-run-of-the-mill family, whose support always warmed her up through life's cold-feet moments. Beth is the author of several books for children, including *Izzy Kline Has Butterflies* and the Starring Jules series. She lives in Port Washington, New York, with her husband and two children. Visit her online at bethain.com.

31901067428682